". . . a story that will best be remembered for its deep and simple tenderness. No one knows as well as Meindert DeJong how a boy loves." *The New York Times*

"This is truly that rare thing, a book you cannot bear to put down . . . memorable . . . brilliantly etched . . . candid realism and gentle humor." *Saturday Review*

". . . [a] memorable book . . . [This] great adventure, vividly evoked by a master storyteller, will hold readers enthralled from first to last." Chicago *Tribune*

". . . a charming book . . ." *Childhood Education*

"Highly recommended." *Catholic Library World*

"Beautifully written with vivid characterization . . ."
Bulletin of the Center for Children's Books

"A warm story enriched by the author's sense of humor . . ." *The Booklist*

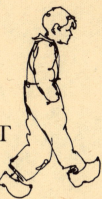

JOURNEY FROM PEPPERMINT STREET

JOURNEY FROM PEPPERMINT STREET

by
MEINDERT
DeJONG

pictures by
EMILY ARNOLD McCULLY

A HARPER TROPHY BOOK
HARPER & ROW, PUBLISHERS
New York, Evanston, San Francisco, London

ALL LITTLE BOOKS GO TO MARKET
BUT THIS ONE IS FOR FRED.

TO FREDERICK TEN HOOR

JOURNEY FROM PEPPERMINT STREET

Text copyright © 1968 by Meindert DeJong
Pictures copyright © 1968 by Emily Arnold McCully

First published in 1968. 5th printing, 1970.
First Harper Trophy Book printing, 1971.

SBN 06–440011–5

Contents

The toad beneath the harrow knows
Exactly where each tooth-point goes.

RUDYARD KIPLING

JOURNEY
FROM
PEPPERMINT
STREET

1

Song of the Seven Frogs and Seven Larks

Siebren held Knillis's hand high so Mother could see it as they walked away. Knillis's little hand fitted into the middle of Siebren's hand. That was because Knillis was the little brother—seven whole years and five months younger. Father always said, "Now, Siebren, remember when I'm not home you're the big one around here." Father was always building new schools and churches and houses in other villages, so he was gone a lot.

Mother never said anything about Siebren's being the big one. Couldn't she see that he was holding Knillis's hand tight? Then why did she still have to stand there in the middle of Peppermint Street and call out so everyone could hear: "Keep holding Knillis's hand. Walk nicely that way, but don't go outside the village, you hear?"

Siebren didn't answer, and Knillis couldn't. Knillis knew only one word that wasn't even a word—*Da*. He called out *Da* to everyone in the whole village— even to big people, even to dogs.

Siebren wasn't scared of dogs because with Knillis he had to be the big one around the whole village too. And if you walked softly dogs mostly didn't notice you. But Knillis had to call out his *Da*, and then the dogs would stop and look. Of course Siebren was too big to be afraid of dogs—but still it was a little bit awful to have dogs stand there and wait for you!

There Mother still stood watching. And Knillis kept saying *Da* to a cat in the windowsill of a house they were passing, even though the cat was sleeping. But Knillis wanted the cat to see his new wooden shoes. They were black, and they had gold buttons painted on them because they were baby shoes. Siebren's old wooden shoes were all bleached out and had no color left at all. One was cracked, and it had fine wire stapled over the top to keep it from splitting in two when he ran hard over the cobblestone streets.

Siebren dragged Knillis away from the house of the cat. If Mother was going to keep standing and

2

standing there, he wanted to duck into the alley between Father's carpenter shop and Father's low, long sand-and-gravel shed.

Boy, you sure didn't feel very big when your mother had to stand watching you out of sight. Siebren watched Mother out of the corner of his eye, then swung into the alley so fast he all but pulled Knillis out of his gold-button shoes.

When they came out of the narrow dark alley they were in the sunny street that ran between the dike and the church. Here there were no houses and nobody for Knillis to call out *Da* to, for the church was high and long and the dike was high and longer.

As they walked past the church they were still in the village, but the street went on outside the village. Of course, the dike went on too, for dikes have no end. Dikes have to go around all the oceans and seas to keep the water off the land, as anybody would know except maybe Knillis.

Outside the village the dike-church street became a gravel road, and their shoes began making great crish-creesh-crunch sounds in the loose gravel. It was almost as if the gravel were making hurt, angry sounds under their hard-stepping wooden shoes.

Knillis didn't know they were going out of the village because they were still walking past a barn. But the barn was the last thing in the village. Now before

them was only the flat, straight road going through endless flat fields. Beside the road there was nothing but the dike following the endless sea.

In the stillness and emptiness Knillis began to look as if he were going to cry. Maybe Siebren was holding Knillis's hand too tight.

"Was I hurting you?" Siebren asked in his nicest big-brother voice. They stood still, and his voice was the only sound in the big empty stillness. Siebren tugged Knillis on. It was better to make crunching noises in the gravel.

The white road went straight, but far in the distance the green dike turned away from the white gravel road. It went on its own high, humped way— it had to—because dikes have to follow the sea wherever it goes. But now in the empty flatness there was one other thing, a deep pond straight ahead.

Siebren wasn't supposed to take Knillis near deep water. He wasn't supposed to go near deep water himself. But the pond seemed friendly and safe because seven frogs were singing and booming there. Oh, maybe there were more than seven, maybe seventy-seven, but Siebren could count seven separate boomings. He counted very loud; he held Knillis's hand tight.

The water pond would have seemed more dangerous if it hadn't been for the seven frogs booming.

5

Then because of the crunching through the gravel seven skylarks rose out of the deep grass between the road and the pond. They rose so high in the sky that they became seven singing dots. Those seven little dots sang all the stillness out of the whole sky above the stretching silent fields and road. Then Knillis began to call his *Da*'s up to the larks and down to the frogs in the pond. It made everything friendlier than friendly, and easy—and Mother didn't know a thing about any of it.

On the far side of the pond on top of the dike was a stack of piled-up narrow rails, and this was the real reason Siebren had come here. He had thought of it in bed early this morning. In bed in his mind the stacked rails on the dike had looked as if they were the freight car of a train. But here piled up before him on the dike they still looked that way—the piled tracks did look like a train. "Shall we go and play train on those tracks on the dike?" he asked Knillis eagerly.

Knillis's eyes got big, but of course he was so small he didn't know anything about trains. It was a wonderful idea just the same—the piled tracks on the dike would be the train, but the brick path that ran along the top of the whole dike would be the track! The brick path would be train tracks, but the tracks themselves would be the train. It was all twisted around and cuckoo and wonderful. Siebren sighed.

Oh, he wished he could tell Knillis how funny and twisted it was, but Knillis was too small to understand anything.

As they climbed the dike Siebren wished again that Knillis weren't so much younger. Then he could tell him that here where the tracks were piled was the exact spot where the sea had tried to break through the dike and go thundering over the land. Why, if the dike had broken, fish would have gone swimming down all the streets of Weirom—even Peppermint Street, even in and out of their own house through the broken windows, caved in by the sea. That's what Father had said! "If it hadn't been for all that sand and gravel piled high in my shed, the sea would have torn a hole in the dike, then roared through the hole into Weirom, and we'd all have gone under to live with the fish. Luckily it happened that the shed was full of sand, so the fish stayed in the sea."

What if he could tell that to Knillis? Oh he'd like to tell Knillis!

Why, that whole night while the sea was breaking the dike all the men of the village had gone back and forth along the top of the quaking dike with sacks of sand and gravel. They'd thrown sacks and all into the breaking hole. "Everything went into that hole but the shed itself," Father had said. "At last with the coming of daylight there wasn't any hole. Then in the ebb tide the sea pulled back from the dike.

7

Imagine—that whole endless sea held back by my sand and gravel bags!"

Father's sacks of sand had had to hold the sea back until men had come from the Queen's government to rebuild the dike. They had come with mine cars and with stacks of narrow rails for the mine cars. The Queen's men had dug an enormous hole on the land side of the dike. Again and again, day after day, they'd filled the mine cars from the great hole. They'd pushed the mine cars up to fill the break in the dike with rocks and dirt until it was safe and solid, and strong enough to hold back the sea.

Only then had the Queen's men gone away. But they'd left one pile of stacked mine-car rails across the exact spot where the dike had broken. Then the hole the men had dug to fill the break in the dike had slowly become a pond. Now frogs were booming in the pond that once had been a deeply dug hole— a hole that had been made to make the dike whole!

Siebren looked eagerly at Knillis. Oh, that was a good way to say it—a hole to make the dike whole. . . . Aw, Knillis was too young even to know that that was funny. He boosted Knillis up on top of the stack of rails. "Hang on, you," he told Knillis. "If you hang on tight, you can't fall."

Knillis sat high and scared on the crosstie where Siebren had put him. He hung on with both hands, but he wanted to cry. When Siebren climbed up and seated himself on a crosstie facing Knillis, it turned out that Knillis wanted to cry because one of his new gold-button shoes had fallen off. To keep him quiet, Siebren took off his own shoe and let it go banging down the side of the piled-up tracks. Because it was the cracked one it was extra noisy, and it clunked and banged with such a hollow sound it made Knillis laugh. While Knillis was giggling, Siebren hastily called out in a loud train voice: "All aboard on this train. All aboard to America."

Knillis didn't know about America. He just giggled and kicked off his other shoe, making it bang down the stack of tracks. But the little black shoe rolled down the whole dike, all the way to the edge of the pond. Hearing the wooden shoe clump and rattle, the frogs in the pond dived down and were still. But above the pond all seven larks fell out of the sky, as if they too wanted to dive down and be still. Then it was as if everything were listening—the whole sky and all the still fields. But it was as if the stillness really came up out of the deep dangerous pond where the frogs had dived down and the larks had fallen.

In the big silence Knillis started to cry. He opened his mouth so wide and big and round that Siebren, clutching his crosstie, was looking way down into Knillis's throat, and the crying came rushing out at him. Then in that rush of crying it was as if the pile of tracks they were sitting on was rushing away with them along the endless dike.

That scared Siebren. As loud as he could, he yelled

right down into Knillis's wide-open mouth: "Now this train has stopped. Now we're back from America. Now we're going home to Mother—so stop your crying."

At the word "mother" Knillis stopped crying, and Siebren scrambled down from the stack of rails and lifted Knillis down. He pushed the one dropped shoe on Knillis's foot but carried his own dropped shoe in his hand so Knillis wouldn't start crying because he had only one. Each on one wooden shoe and one woolen sock, they limped down the dike to the edge of the pond to get the other black baby shoe. The gold buttons shone friendly in the deep grass, and that was a good thing because the pond stood awfully deep and still.

Siebren shoved Knillis's foot into his shoe as fast as he could, rammed his own foot into his old shoe, and then they ran. Hand in hand they ran hard and breathlessly until at last there was the church and the cobbles. They had to go slowly down the cobbled church street because Knillis's side had started to ache so hard it made him stumbly.

It was a good thing they'd slowed down and looked exactly as if all the time they'd just been walking around in the village because there—beyond the long church—there stood Mother. She came hurrying and grabbed Knillis up to hold him tight and safe—almost as if he and Knillis had really been to America. With Mother not knowing, everything was so safe

11

that for a moment Siebren wanted to push his own face into Mother's thick skirts. But Mother looked down and said, "Siebren, why has Knillis been crying? What did you do to him?"

"Nothing," Siebren said most softly.

For a moment Mother smiled a thin, tight little smile. "Of course, nothing. It's always nothing. I should have known." But luckily she had something else on her mind. "You know why I came out?" she said. "Your father came home. And the first thing when he came home, he asked: 'Where's that big guy, Siebren?' So then I had to go looking for you."

Siebren wanted to run right then, but they were going down the narrow alley between Father's carpenter shop and Father's sand-and-gravel shed. It was a squeeze of an alley; it was almost too narrow for Mother's wide skirts, and she was holding Knillis. Siebren could hardly push Mother's skirts aside to get by her. He couldn't hurry, so then he asked, "Mother, where's America?"

Mother answered by saying, "Look, there's your father now, coming down the alley—he couldn't wait."

Siebren thrust Mother's skirts aside and flew. He grabbed his father's hand. Hand in hand and side by side he and Father walked up the alley that was hardly wide enough for Mother's skirts. Father's hand felt sure and strong around his hand—sure as the

12

dike and strong as the church. Siebren felt so excited and safe he just had to tell or ask his father something. "Dad," he exploded, "can seven larks fall out of the sky down into a pond and drown?"

His father only said, "Golly, Siebren, I'm as glad as seven larks to see you."

But Mother heard Siebren. "Seven larks," she screamed. "Riemer, did you hear that? Seven larks! And look at Knillis's little hands—all rust! They went to that pond way out of the village and played on that dangerous high stack of mine-car rails."

Father still held Siebren's hand securely, but now he stopped and looked down at Siebren hard.

Behind them Mother said, "Against all my orders! Deliberately! The last thing I called out to Siebren was 'Don't go out of the village.' Then he ducked down this alley and went straight to those tracks by that deep pond with his little baby brother."

"Is it true?" Father asked.

Siebren nodded.

"Here I haven't seen you for almost a week, and this is about the lousiest way to greet your son," Father said slowly. "But I guess, Siebren, I've got to greet you with a spanking. And I guess, while I'm guessing, that this is as good a place as any to do it— at least nobody can see us here."

Then Father calmly lifted Siebren off the ground by the hand he was holding, upended him, and spanked him with a big flat work hand that was hard as a stone. In the tight alley there was no other sound but the hard, hurting, stinging slap sounds. There was no other sound because Siebren wouldn't cry.

But then Knillis started to cry instead. Cry! He screamed—screamed and screamed, he was so scared by the spanking. Siebren, upended, could see Knillis raise his scared hands and rub and rub them through his hair. The whole top of Knillis's head turned blotchy and red and rusty from his rusty hands. Knillis wouldn't stop screaming no matter how much Mother shushed and shushed, so Father had to stop spanking.

"You can thank your little brother," Father said between breaths, "simply because I can't have people think I'm here, up a tight dark alley, beating the daylights out of a baby. But, Siebren, you'll admit, won't you, that you had this spanking coming to you?" Father sounded calm and good again, and like Father. He took Siebren's hand once more, and side by side they walked down the alley. Behind them Mother was wiping the top of Knillis's rusty head with the bottom of her flipped-up apron, and Knillis was quiet.

As they started to leave the alley Father said, "Now I'll never have to do that again—I mean, spank you for that?"

"Oh, no," Siebren said.

"Well, don't sound so agreeable about it," Father

14

said. "A man doesn't want a humble-meek, yes-saying little old lady for a son. I expect to have to wallop you for many other things from time to time—but not for deep water! When you can't swim, that doesn't make sense."

Behind them Mother laughed right out and sounded happy. "Think of it!" she told Siebren. "We won't merely have that father of yours the rest of this day, but all day tomorrow—Sunday. We'll have fun . . . but, Siebren, don't worry about the larks. Larks drop from the sky when their songs are finished, but into the grass, not into ponds. Larks have to drop like stones when they have sung all the stillness out of the sky—that's the way it is with larks."

From the alley they stepped into Peppermint Street. Father said, "Did you really honestly see seven larks all together?"

Siebren proudly said, "Seven larks and seven frogs booming."

Father actually looked as though he could hardly believe it. "Seven larks in a bunch! But larks are nearly always alone when singing up in the sky. Seven larks—do you know what that is called? It's an exultation of larks."

Siebren believed it. Because it was an exultation of a day—his father was home, and even the larks were safe—all seven larks. Why, it was almost worth half a spanking!

2

Song of the Cheap, Cheap Caps

In the living room Siebren built blocks into a steep pyramid on the tray of Knillis's high chair and decided that he had the most tedious job in all the world—Knillis! Knillis was the job for all the free hours of every day—before school, between school, and after school—*every* day.

Knillis had been sick again—for the third time! Since that time he and Knillis had gone outside the village and played on the mine-car tracks, Knillis had been sick with pneumonia three times. Oh, but playing on those tracks now seemed long ago!

Now Knillis wasn't sick, but *now* he had a head

that itched like fiery sin. He had to have thick mittens on his hands so he couldn't scratch the rusty itch. The doctor had ordered them.

Before those three sicknesses he and Knillis had walked way outside the village to the pond. And they'd run all the way back. Now Knillis couldn't run—couldn't walk—all he could do was sit in a high chair.

Last week Mother had said right out—she was so hopeless—that if Knillis was sick much more, he would stay an eternal baby. Well, if that happened, then he, Siebren, would have an eternal, dreary, tedious, unending job. It was no fun.

Siebren felt so mean inside that he made Knillis wait before he placed the topmost block on the high pyramid. Knillis sat scowling, so closely he watched. Siebren scowled right back. But there—all in one hard swat—Knillis sent the blocks flying over the room.

"Is that all you can ever do?" Siebren asked. "Now what's the fun of that? You can't walk, you can't talk, all you can do is go SWAT."

The words felt dry and sour in his mouth. He heard himself—he sounded almost as if he were crying. Now one by slow one he'd have to pick up the blocks, then one by slow one build them up again. Then one short single SWAT!

"Is that all you can do?" Siebren asked once more from the floor as he picked up the scattered blocks.

It was Monday—washday. But Mother had had to wait until he got home from school to start the washing—all because of Knillis. Siebren crawled toward the doorway to pick up the blocks that had gone way out there. There stood Mother. She must have been standing there all the time. She picked up a block. "Siebren," she said reproachfully, "is that a way to talk to a baby?"

Right then Siebren did not care. He got up, looked at Mother, and dumped the blocks on the high-chair tray. Because he did not start building blocks right away Knillis started screaming. But for once Mother let Knillis scream. She pulled up a chair and sat down opposite Siebren. "I guess the time has come when I've got to explain a little more," Mother said.

Knillis began to scream so loud that Mother had to yell into Siebren's ear. "You've got to understand, because you're going to have to take care of Knillis even more. You see—Mother's going to have a baby."

Mother had to shout so loud about the new baby that she got a little bit pink and funny in the face. Her hair was all steamy from the wash. Right then Siebren didn't care a thing about the new baby. "Why does Knillis want to do nothing but swat blocks? I build them up nice and try to make forts and castles, but all he does is SWAT. Now what's the fun of that? SWAT!"

"Didn't you hear me?" Mother asked, surprised. "Don't you mind about another baby?"

"Just so it doesn't have a sore head," Siebren said sourly. "No. It's just always having to take care of Knillis before and after school."

"I know," Mother said, and she could say it softly because—for no reason—Knillis was suddenly quiet. "I know," she repeated, "but he's been sick so much, and now he's so miserable with his little head. It itches so terribly he doesn't get any rest. Day and night that fiery itch—and he's too little to understand. So you try to understand, Siebren. Try to imagine your head on fire all day and night. I wouldn't just knock blocks to the floor. I'd throw them through the window—through all the windows."

Siebren started to laugh because he thought Mother was making a joke, but Mother looked solemn, and Knillis sat solemnly staring at her. She jumped up, pulled Knillis out of his high chair, and sat down with him in her lap. She was so loving she rested her chin over the top of Knillis's head. How he felt must have shown in Siebren's face for Mother laughed. "Don't look so squeamish, Siebren," she said. "It's just a dry scale in his hair. It almost looks like rust, doesn't it?"

In the kitchen the washboiler boiled over. The dirty soapsuds on the hot stove smelt so bad that Mother pushed Knillis into Siebren's arms and ran to the kitchen. Siebren sat still. He sat scared. Now Mother had seen too that it looked like rust. It was rust! The rust from the long ago mine-car rails.

Mother hadn't remembered about his taking Knillis to play on the mine-car rails. She hadn't remembered that Knillis had rubbed the rust all through his hair there in the alley when Father had spanked him— Siebren—so hard.

No, Mother hadn't remembered, but the next day Knillis was sick. Then he'd been sick twice more, and now after all that sickness, the rust was coming back out of his head.

It was awesome to be the only one to know. He hadn't told because he had hoped he was wrong, but now he was sure. Now even Mother had seen it was rust. He still couldn't tell, and he never would. Never! Instead he'd take the best care of Knillis and never complain or be sour or mean with Knillis again. Never —in all his life!

Siebren wrestled Knillis up in the high chair as gently as he could. "Shall I build blocks for you?" he asked in his kindest voice. "You can knock them right down again. You can knock them through the windows—all the windows." He laughed to show Knillis it was meant to be a joke.

Knillis looked at him. Suddenly he raised his mittened hand as if he were going to swat Siebren hard, the way he swatted the blocks. Siebren had to hold Knillis's hands between his own to keep them down. He suddenly thought they looked as if they had their hands folded to pray. Knillis was so still it seemed right to pray, and Siebren prayed right out, fast:

20

"Please, God, cure the rust on Knillis's head, for Jesus's sake, amen." Then he added as an afterthought —it didn't belong in the prayer—"Then I'll never have to tell."

As if in answer to the prayer there came a knock on the door that thundered through the hall. Somebody started to sing. Then Siebren knew it was Pieter Klimstra, who sold caps from door to door out of a big velvet bag and sang a song about his caps at every house. Now he threw the top half of their door open and sang into the hall:

> *Klimstra's caps they are so cheap,*
> *So dirt cheap, so dirt cheap,*
> *Klimstra's caps they are so cheap—*
> *Even Klimstra can hardly believe it!*

Siebren hesitated whether to go to the door or run and tell Mother. When he'd been little, he'd been terribly scared of the velvet bag. Mothers always told little kids that if they were naughty, Pieter Klimstra would take them away in the black bag. When you were little you believed it. Mothers said that Pieter Klimstra went into the whole wide world selling his caps, and there you'd go into the world inside a black velvet bag.

While Siebren hesitated Mother came hurrying from the kitchen to let Pieter Klimstra in. When they came into the living room Mother was saying,

21

"Well, Mister Klimstra, yes, I guess we could stand a new cap for Siebren."

"Knillis too," Siebren urged softly. "One for Knillis too. Then nobody can see his sore head."

"No, his little head needs the air and the sunshine," Mother said. It made Pieter Klimstra look at Knillis. Then, unexpectedly, he swung the bulging black bag down from his shoulder right onto Siebren's toes. Siebren didn't pull back because that would show he was still scared of the velvet bag, but just the same he shivered a little inside.

When Pieter Klimstra opened the bag there was— of course—nothing in it but caps. Pieter Klimstra stirred around in the mess of caps as if they were so much porridge, but when he pulled one out and put it on Siebren's head, it fit! Imagine, Pieter Klimstra had known just which cap in the whole bag would fit. And Mother liked the cap so much she bought it without even wanting to look at another. It was like magic.

Mother was going to pay for the cap, but Pieter Klimstra didn't take the money. Instead he reached into his pocket and brought out a small jar of salve. He said the salve would heal Knillis's head if anything could. He said it was MAGIC SALVE.

Mother listened and studied the print on the jar, but she looked doubtful. Then Pieter Klimstra reached into his other pocket and handed Mother a small tin of chocolates. There were tiny soft-pink roses on the cover of the little tin. Pieter Klimstra said the chocolates were for Knillis, and they were free—as some comfort for the poor baby—but wouldn't Mother like the salve for the poor one's little head?

Mother still looked doubtful, but she bought the jar of salve—then Pieter Klimstra took the money.

After he left, Mother immediately took the cap off Siebren's head and put it on the table. It was for Sundays. Then she decided that the chocolates ought to be for Sunday too. And even though Pieter Klimstra had given them for Knillis, they'd all have the chocolates on Sunday—as a comfort—in case Father didn't get home.

It was a disappointment, but the next disappointment was worse. Mother didn't put the new salve on Knillis's head. Instead she took it and locked it in the living-room highboy. Siebren sat in utter frustration—he had so planned to watch the salve heal Knillis's head. Place a block, head heal a little; place another slow block, head heal a little more; another block, another heal. Oh, it would be exciting! He'd build the blocks as slowly as possible, and then suddenly the whole head would be healed—like magic and the answer to a prayer.

With the salve locked up, Mother had gone back to the kitchen, and now with the excitement of Pieter Klimstra's visit all gone, there was nothing to do but build blocks again. The day became as dreary and un-magic as any other day.

Siebren dragged out the building of a pyramid. Knillis sat scowling, mittened hand ready. Siebren began singing Pieter Klimstra's song of the cheap, cheap caps. Over and over he sang the song, one slow dragged-out word for each slow block. Slowly, monot-onously, he droned the whole song over and over.

He wasn't aware he'd been singing the song until Mother called out from the kitchen: "Siebren! Will you stop singing that awful, tuneless song about the cheap, cheap caps? You're singing me to sleep over the washtub. Do you want me to drown among the diapers?"

Siebren clamped his mouth shut in surprise, com-pletely unaware he'd been singing the song over and over. He grinned about Mother's joke of drowning in diapers, but Knillis scowled, so then Siebren put up a slow block. But the moment he lifted the block the dreary song started itself too. It began of itself, it sang itself—Siebren couldn't seem to help it. He half expected that any moment he'd get a wet slap from his mother's wash hand, but still the song wouldn't quit. It sang itself; it insisted on singing itself—in spite of him!

The last block was on the tippety-top of the tottery pyramid, and the song ended. Siebren hastily pulled back so Knillis wouldn't knock any blocks in his

25

face. Nothing happened. Nothing happened because Knillis sat sound asleep in the high chair!

Unbelieving, all excited, Siebren slid from his chair and stole to the kitchen. He didn't dare even whisper. He beckoned to Mother with a hushing, crooked finger. Mother tiptoed after him to the living room. There sat Knillis sound asleep.

Mother made unbelieving sounds. "Why, he hasn't slept like that in weeks," she whispered. Then she was afraid to make another sound.

Siebren and Mother slipped back to the kitchen. There Mother sighed such a great gushing sigh of relief she blew a big gap in the steam over the wash-tub. Through the gap Siebren looked at her. "Now may I go out and play?"

Mother started to nod permission, then suddenly caught herself. "Oh, Siebren," she said mournfully, "I'm on the last tubful, and late as it is, I was hoping still to hang out the wash. It's so clear, windy, and sunny."

She saw Siebren's face. "Oh, I know, I know—why, it's a miracle almost. . . . Listen, I'll tell you what. While I hang out the wash you go and sit with Knillis and have that whole tin of chocolates all for yourself—just you alone. Then as soon as I've hung up the wash you can play. But save the little tin for me, hunh? Those little roses on the cover are so pretty."

Siebren turned away fast. He had to swallow hard, he was so disappointed.

In the living room Knillis still sat sleeping, but Siebren felt so mean he grabbed the chocolate tin and jerked the hinged cover up so angrily hard he almost cut his finger. In fact, it sliced a sliver off the tip of his thumbnail. He took the opened tin and let the whole layer of tiny chocolates slide into his mouth right from the box. With his big mouthful, he went to sit down in front of the sleeping Knillis.

In spite of how hateful he felt, the chocolates tasted good. Why, they were extra good this way—a whole propping, jammed, melting mouthful. Oh it was good! The melting chocolate slid down his throat in long, thick trickles. He rubbed his lips and looked down at his smeary fingers. When he looked up again, Knillis's eyes were open. There he sat with his mouth full of Knillis's chocolates. There wasn't even one left in the tin. He stared down into the open tin box and swallowed and swallowed to get rid of the chocolates.

Sunlight coming through the window caught the golden inside of the tin and reflected a bright quivery spot on the ceiling. Siebren looked toward the sunny window and was surprised to see Mother already hanging up the washing on the big wooden clotheshorse she had carried into the street. With Siebren's twisting around to watch Mother, the chocolate tin, quite by accident, reflected a little dancing sunbeam on

Knillis's nose. Knillis looked cross-eyed at the shimmering spot and tried to catch it with his mittened hand. Siebren laughed and called out to Mother to show her how nicely he was entertaining Knillis.

"Oh, did he wake up?" Mother asked. Then she was looking down the street. "Oh, oh," she called out. "Now wouldn't you know it! There now comes that miserable miller of Nes with his loaded flour wagon. Why must that man always deliver flour to Peppermint Street on washdays?"

It was Monday—washday—and there were clotheshorses down Peppermint Street all the way to the village square. Mother turned and screeched a shrill hallooing call to warn all the other women—the little street was simply too narrow for clotheshorses and live horses, and then still a wagon loaded high with bags of flour.

Siebren ran to the window. Now the warning of the coming wagon went screaming down Peppermint Street from house to house. Women came flutter-running from everywhere, stooped under their huge wooden clotheshorses, picked them up, and ran with them in one long bobbing white line to the village square.

Siebren squeezed flat-nosed and slant-eyed against the window to watch it all. After three tries the long, loaded wagon managed the turn into narrow Peppermint Street. The horses came on. Then the sight of the bobbing, flapping clotheshorses scared the real horses and made them back out of the street. But the miller whipped them on, and on they came.

Mother was last in the long row of bobbing clothes. But now she wasn't Mother anymore—she was a giant wooden ridge-backed ostrich scuttling from charging horses. There was nothing to be seen of her but her wooden shoes. Behind her the horses came pounding, and their iron shoes rang and struck fire out of the cobbles.

Suddenly, right before the window, the horses took fright again. Both reared up as one, hoofs pawing, nostrils snorting and blowing, eyes bulged white with fear. The near horse twisted and plunged up so wildly his one iron hoof appeared in the window, came down, and struck sparks from the stone windowsill. Siebren fell back, but behind him Knillis burbled and giggled and blew bubbles of excitement. When Siebren looked back from Knillis, the miller of Nes had his horses under control, the women were gone into the village square, and the long wagon rolled heavily on toward the bakery.

Knillis started screaming. He liked the horses; he wanted more horses striking sparks out of the window-sill. He screamed for the horses. To quiet him, Siebren hastily shone the bright inside of the tin at him. "See—see," he said and walked toward Knillis, making a sunbeam spot dance all over him.

"See—see?" He stood right before the high chair and ran the sunny spot down Knillis's stubby nose. Suddenly Knillis grabbed the chocolate tin with both mittened hands. It closed—but Siebren's thumb was between the razor-sharp edge of the box and the cover! It cut. A pain, sharp-thin as the razor-sharp edge of the box, stabbed through Siebren's thumb, shot up his arm. It hurt—oh horribly! For a moment Siebren stood just staring at Knillis. Then with all his scared, hurt might he screamed into Knillis's face. Knillis only screamed back and clamped his hands still harder down on the tin.

"Knillis, let go. No, Knillis. PLEASE, no." Siebren's knees quaked as he pray-whispered the sick, scared words.

Knillis's eyes popped out with his screaming, and the harder he screamed, the harder he pinched. The sharp tin sawed down into Siebren's thumb. Desperately he hit Knillis on top of his bowed head —slapped him again and again until he let go. The chocolate tin clattered to the floor.

Siebren sagged down on the chair before Knillis's high chair, sat sick as the thumb bled and bled. Knillis was howling because he'd been slapped, but he leaned over his tray, looked at the tin on the floor, and was still. Siebren pushed Knillis's head back and laid his own head on the tray. He was very tired. His hand hung down, and blood dripped.

When Siebren glanced down and saw the blood, he had to get down on his knees and be sick on the floor. Shamed, scared, wretched, he stooped low to the floor and was sick again. The room was getting dim.

There came a pounding in the dim, dark room. Siebren couldn't look up, but he somehow knew the noise was Mother. Floods of relief washed over him. Everything would be right now—everything. He tried to get to his feet, and Mother helped him. Her body heaved against his from her hard running. He could hear her swallowing to get her breath. He tried to explain what had happened. His words wouldn't fit together, and at the same time Mother was saying fierce things under her breath—over and over—the same thing.

Mother was terribly angry, but he couldn't explain; the words wouldn't fit. Through the dimness it came to him that Mother was angry with herself—so angry she stamped the chocolate tin to a flat nothing on the floor. . . . She wasn't angry with him! Luxuriantly he leaned against her. Things were going dark, but it was all right; Mother was holding him. He fainted and slid into darkness.

3

Song of the Hungry Goats

When Siebren came to, the first thing he heard was
Mother sucking in her breath. She had found him
too heavy to lift off the floor, but she had pulled
his hand straight up to slow the bleeding.

"I heard you both screaming from way down in
the square," she said. "Now, of course, Knillis sits
there sleeping, but oh, it was scary, that screaming. I
shouldn't run, but I ran and ran . . . your poor thumb
—oh, Siebren."

When Mother said that, he started to cry—but
that was because he felt so weak. Through hard sobs
he told her what had happened. He remembered he
had slapped Knillis on the head, but he didn't tell

her that. He did explain, "I guess Knillis got scared because I screamed. The scareder he got, the harder he pinched. He was so scared he couldn't let go."

"Don't go over it," Mother said. "You'll just get sick again." She helped him up from the floor. He had to hold on to the edge of a chair with his good hand, he was so dizzy.

"Now sit down, shut your eyes, and don't look at the blood. But keep your hand up," Mother ordered. "I'll get bandages from the kitchen."

Siebren was only too glad to shut his eyes, he was so light-headed. But after a while it was strange—it felt as if somebody were standing over him. He knew Mother was in the kitchen. He opened his eyes.

It was Grandpa! His grandfather had come into the house, and there he stood, silently looking at Siebren's thumb. Mother came back. "Father," she said, surprised, and from that began explaining in a flood of words about the accident.

Siebren started to sway on the chair. Grandpa saw it, reached over to the table, took the coffeepot, and without a word tilted the spout into Siebren's mouth. Cold coffee trickled down both sides of his chin, but just like that the cold, bitter coffee straightened his tumbling stomach and steadied his eyes. He looked up. "Why is Grandpa here?"

"Siebren!" Mother said.

"He's right to ask," Grandpa said. "I come so seldom, even though it's just across the village. It seems

34

the only time I come is to report an emergency. But this time Siebren seems to have the emergency waiting for me." He studied the cut. "Some thumb," he said roughly. "It's just about the size of two thumbs now. But you'll be all right, Siebren. It's a neat, clean cut. Why, I can promise you it'll be better long before you're an old woman."

It was some sort of rough big-man joke, Siebren knew. He tried to laugh. Instead silly tears came into his eyes. To hide the tears he asked, "Did Grandpa come because of my thumb?"

"No," Grandpa said promptly. "I'm here to leave your mother the key to my house so she can feed the cat while I go visit my sister Anna. I just got word she's very sick and not expected to live. Of course when I visit Sister Anna, I'll stop in at your inland aunt's monastery too."

Siebren hadn't even known he had an inland aunt. Oh, it sounded strange—an aunt in a monastery! It sounded so strange he blurted right out, "May I go with you, Grandpa?"

He'd never have dared if it hadn't been that he'd just cut his thumb.

Mother stopped her bandaging and stared at him. But Grandpa simply said, "Well, why not?"

Then, amazingly, · Mother said, "Oh, it'd be good for Siebren. He's always with Knillis, and now this. . . ."

Siebren sucked in his breath and let it out whistling. There it was, this moment, the greatest thing in his life. He'd never been out of the village—oh, except to the next village of Nes—and here he was going to an inland aunt in a monastery.

Mother and Grandfather had begun talking about the trip; Siebren sat still and unbelieving. He was so grateful he could have burst. And it was Knillis who had made it all happen. Oh, it was almost worth a sore thumb. His eye fell on the chocolate tin that Mother had stamped to a flat nothing. He was off his chair and grabbing the tin. The next moment, shaking with the effort, he rammed it out of sight in his back pocket. It was flat and bloody; that didn't matter at all—it was good luck. Maybe it was magic; hadn't it brought the great trip?

Siebren slid onto his chair just as Grandfather and Mother turned to look at him, but their minds were on their talk. Then Mother said to Grandpa, "You mean now? You mean go this late in the day? Why, it'll be pitch-black when you get to that awful marsh at the monastery."

"I shouldn't wait," Grandfather said. "Sister Anna is old. She's very sick. No, I wouldn't want to wait. And night's a good time for journeying."

"Oh, now I don't know," Mother fretted. "All that blood he's lost—he even fainted. . . ."

Siebren sat so tense that he could almost hear his thumb throbbing. He hid the bandaged thumb behind his back.

Grandfather saw it. "Keep that thumb up," he ordered. But it was Mother he was impatient with. "You know," he told her, "it's stopped bleeding now, and with a kid, the moment it's over he's chipper again. The fresh air will straighten him out, and it isn't as if we were going to darkest Africa—it's just to the monastery and a little beyond. It's just one night. If everything is well, we'll come stamping home again some time tomorrow."

"But what about his thumb? What if it gives trouble? The whole countryside asleep, only you two about, and Siebren bleeding and bleeding."

"I don't expect any trouble," Grandfather said. "If necessary, I can bandage it again. Just give me a couple of clean rags to take along. We'll manage."

Mother looked at Siebren's raised hand. "Well," she said doubtfully, "if you've just got to go . . . but Siebren can't walk with his hand held up like a wooden semaphore—I'll have to fix a sling."

Mother started for the kitchen, but she turned back. "While I fix a sling and some sandwiches will you help Siebren get dressed in his Sunday suit?" she asked. She gave Siebren a lovely big smile. "Sure, Siebren, you're going. Don't look so worried. You've certainly earned a trip, and I'll manage. Why, I'll do just like you. I'll sing that cheap-cap song so often that the only way Knillis can get away from it is by going to sleep." She grinned at Siebren.

He wanted to hug her, but she was already going

to the kitchen, and anyhow he'd better help Grandpa with the Sunday clothes. He felt sure that once he was dressed Mother couldn't possibly change her mind. He found his clothes for Grandpa.

Oh, but he'd never get dressed. He was clumsy with just one hand, and Grandpa was just as clumsy at helping him. Finally when Grandpa kneeled to tie the laces on his Sunday leather shoes, Siebren leaned far out and snatched the new Pieter Klimstra cap off the table. He pulled it tight over his head—a cap was always the last thing to put on—it made you feel all ready, and almost sure to go.

Mother came at last. She began to fit the sling she'd made around Siebren's neck. When he looked down at the girlish scarf he didn't say a thing; he even tried not to look disappointed. She had made the sling from her prettiest scarf, but it had little red roses all over it. They were almost like the roses on the choco-late tin. He mustn't forget the tin! It was luck.

Grandpa was stuffing one of his coat pockets full of sandwiches and the other full of strips of white cloth for bandages. Suddenly he pulled most of the cloths out again and threw them on the table. "Siebren didn't cut off both arms," he grumped.

"You'll be only too grateful for all of them if the thumb starts bleeding again," Mother said. "There you'll be, going through the black swamp in the dark."

"I'll be only too thankful if I can walk. Rags, sand-wiches, what-not—I'll be so loaded it'll end up with Siebren—sore thumb and all—having to carry me the last seven miles to the monastery."

Now Grandpa looked at the sling. "Too fancy womanish with all those red flowers," he grumbled. "And too flimsy too. Look, it needs to be so his hand is strapped to his shoulder so he won't move it around and start it bleeding again."

Siebren had to stand before Grandpa while he tightened and shortened and reknotted the scarf. Grandpa was doing it in such a way that the fewest roses would show. Siebren was grateful—but he'd almost have gone in a girl's dress just so he could go on the trip, just so they could get going!

While Grandpa fitted the sling Mother made believe she was fussing with Siebren's coat—instead she stuffed extra bandages in his pocket. Then at last Grandpa and Mother were ready. They started down the hall. Siebren did not follow but ran back and whipped the flattened tin from his old trousers and rammed it into the back pocket of his Sunday suit. It was pretty bloody, but that didn't matter—it was luck. He was still a little dizzy but hurried after Mother and Grandpa so they wouldn't ask what he had been doing. It was even better luck if the little tin was a secret.

Outside on the stoop Mother was giving last instructions to Grandpa about giving her regards to the people at the monastery. She told Siebren to be a good boy. "And don't you be pesky and peskily pester your grandfather with all kinds of questions." She kissed him.

Siebren said, "No, Mother. Oh no, Mother!"

Mother thought of something else she wanted Grandpa to tell the inland aunt. She cautioned Grandpa not to forget. Grandfather imitated Siebren's voice and said: "No, Mother. Oh no, Mother. Never!"

Then they were lucky because Knillis started crying. "Bye then," Mother said. "Both of you have a good trip and a good time. And both of you be good boys!"

Good boys! Oh, that had been a nice way for Mother to say a last thing. He and Grandpa went down the stoop and stepped into the street, laughing. Laughing, Siebren took the first big step of his great journey into the world. Then Grandpa spoiled it all by saying, "Oh, Siebren, I left my journeying cane behind in the hall."

Back in the hall Siebren heard Mother and Knillis in the living room. He wanted to get going on the journey, but he suddenly wanted just as hard to rush into the living room and kiss Mother and Knillis good-bye. Grandpa coughed in the street. He sounded impatient. Siebren grabbed the cane and ran out of the house.

Stretching his stride to Grandfather's long steps,

Siebren tried to walk down Peppermint Street as straight and sturdy as Grandpa, but he couldn't quite manage it. He had to take a hop and skip now and then just to keep up. But then he did have a sore thumb, and his whole arm was in a sling! Everybody must notice. Everybody must think he looked like a wounded soldier coming home from the wars.

Then it began happening as Siebren was dream-hoping it. In the windows of the houses on both sides of Peppermint Street the curtains began stirring and parting as women inquisitively peered out at him and Grandpa. At the sight of the sling one woman forgot to let the curtain drop back. She just stared openly.

Grandfather noticed it. He looked back, saw they were out of sight of Siebren's house, and said, "Here, let me take that silly sling off. Take my cane instead. Put the cane on your shoulder and hold it with your sore hand—that'll automatically keep your thumb up. All those red roses—you'd think we were crippling back from some bloody battle."

The cane was even better than the sling. The way Grandfather had laid it over his shoulder, he was now a wounded soldier with his gun still in his wounded, bandaged hand. It was even better than that, because this was Grandfather's *journeying* cane. Of course he, Siebren, wasn't really journeying yet. You weren't honestly, truly journeying when you were still in your own village. But the moment he stepped beyond the

41

farthest wall of the farthest house in Weirom his journeying would begin. That moment, that step. And it was going to be the biggest step he could possibly take.

Siebren whistled softly. Imagine, in that one big splitting, spread-eagling step he'd change from a Weirom boy into a journeying stranger.

The last house in the village was the house of Japik Maaikus. Japik's tiny farm was so crowded against the village his barn had to be built right onto the house. Siebren watched it, slant-eyed. You had to be honest about it, had to be fair—the barn was part of the house, so the big step had to be the first step past the barn—not the house. Here it was. Siebren slid his foot forward through the deep, loose gravel. It had to be a step that would almost split him in two. Then the goats of Japik Maaikus heard the gravel rattling and yammered out at him. It was easy to know at that exciting moment just what the trembly goat voices were saying. Just like that, he made up the whole goat song.

Ba-ah, Siebren—journeyer, stranger.
Out in the wide world, Siebren,
Out in the wide, wide world.
But not in a black velvet bag,
Oh, not in a black, ba-ah, bag.
But ba-ah, by-eh, Siebren.
Ba-ah, by-eh, by-eh—journeyer, stranger.

Then Grandfather spoiled the whole song. "Japik is late again feeding his goats," he said disgustedly. "Feeding a little later each day, he now and then saves out a feeding, the miserable old miser."

With his stern disapproving words Grandfather had made the weeping-goat song ordinary and everyday. Of course, Grandfather didn't know that he was talking to a stranger who knew nothing about this village of Weirom or about a man named Japik Maaikus who had hungry goats. The goats still bleated on and on, but what could that mean to him—some old goats in a wayside barn!

Everything was somehow spoiled. It wasn't only Grandpa, but the village too. It wasn't fair. He'd stepped his big splitting step, he'd become a journeying stranger, but Weirom kept following him. Now the clock in the village tower struck six and bonged the sounds out after him. Siebren kept his back fiercely turned, but he couldn't keep out the familiar sound. The goats had stopped bleating to listen to the clock; the clock stopped bonging its six heavy notes, but now the wash and throb of the sea in full tide up against the dike drummed in Siebren's ears.

There was nothing to do but make up some other way of becoming a journeying stranger. Listening to the sea sounds behind him, Siebren discovered an exciting thing. If he grabbed the cane on his shoulder hard with his sore hand, the sound of the sea's surge drumming in his ears was timed exactly to the throb of his thumb under the tight bandage. Hey, it must be that there was a tide in his blood like the tide in the sea. So it must be that when at last he would get so far from the dike and the village that the drum-throb of the sea would no longer beat along with the blood throb in his thumb, then he'd really be a journeying stranger. He'd be an inland stranger going to an inland aunt.

Grandpa turned. "Hey dreamer, you sure are beginning to lag behind."

Siebren, shocked into awareness of Grandpa, hastily mumbled, "Thumb hurts." It was a little bit true, of course, but he'd had to say something mighty fast to keep Grandpa from knowing about his fine inside game.

"Hurt bad?" Grandpa looked at the cane. "Well then, ease up that fierce hold on your cane! The way you're grabbing it, you'd think you had to slay dragons. I don't see any dragons coming at us."

Siebren, quick to pick up the game that must be in Grandfather's mind, grinned and said, "But don't you see that big dragon there behind Nes?" He pointed to the high windmill that towered over the far side of the distant village.

"The windmill?" Grandpa asked. "Siebren, you know that's only the miller of Nes opening up the four wings of his mill so he can do a little grinding by the evening breeze."

"I know," Siebren said, "but that's no fun—that's ordinary."

He dropped behind, hurt that Grandfather could think he wouldn't know about a windmill. *He* hadn't thought up the dragon stuff—Grandpa had. He'd just pointed out the windmill to help out with the dragon game. Big people—when kids looked dreamy—always expected kids to say things like they imagined windmills were dragons. He'd never thought about dragons in his life. He wouldn't know a dragon from a heap of potatoes!

Siebren, disgusted, turned around and started to walk backward. Then he gasped out in delight. "Grandpa," he yelled. "Look! On the dike! Mother and Knillis followed us out of Weirom."

Grandpa looked. "Mackerels!" he said. "Hope your mother can't see you're not wearing the sling. Better face this way—women always fuss and worry."

Siebren had to obey, but his eyes smarted. He looked over his shoulder. Now Mother held Knillis high, and with her hand she made Knillis wave his hand. Siebren waved and waved at her. She'd come with Knillis as far as the pond and the stack of mine-car rails on top of the dike. It was windy on the dike. Mother pointed to her skirts blowing and flapping, then she pointed to Knillis's head. It must mean that the wind wasn't good for Knillis. With a last quick wave, Mother walked down the seaside slope of the

45

dike and was gone. Suddenly the dike stretched lonely and empty all the way back to Weirom. There was no one.

Siebren couldn't stand it. He whirled and tore after his marching grandfather. "Grandpa?" he called out before he had thought what to say. "Grandpa, there's all those rails still piled up on the dike, but the dike's been fixed long ago, and the rails were already rusty when Knillis and I played on them, and Knillis rubbed the rust in his hair. . . ." He stopped, appalled. There, just for something to say, he'd almost told Grandpa the secret about the rust having gone into Knillis's head.

Grandpa looked back at the rails, then he looked at Siebren as if expecting him to say more. Siebren didn't know what to do. "Grandpa," he said hurriedly, "I—I guess I never knew I had an inland aunt."

"Maybe that's because she's really your mother's aunt—she's your *great*-aunt."

"Oh?" Siebren pondered it. "I didn't know I had any aunts—great or small," he said at last. He said it smartly, because it was supposed to be a bright little joke.

"Your great-aunt is a small aunt," Grandpa answered mysteriously. It turned out from Grandfather's grin that this was supposed to be a joke too. "As a matter of fact," Grandfather explained, "your *great-*

46

aunt isn't a bit taller than you. But the reason you haven't any aunts of your own is because your mother was my only child."

"You didn't have any boys—just a girl?"

Grandpa nodded most solemnly. "Sickening, isn't it?" he said. He laughed and laughed then walked away, taking big, hard, amused steps.

Siebren stopped in the road. He forgot to laugh with Grandpa because he was suddenly full of questions. "Why didn't I ever see my great-aunt?" he called out.

Grandpa stopped. "Well, she's a bit of a distance inland and lives on a busy farm, and our lives are sea lives."

It was a strange, mysterious saying, but Grandfather sometimes talked in mysterious old-fashioned ways. Siebren seethed with questions, then he remembered that Mother had warned him not to be pesky and peskily pester Grandpa with questions. She'd said it funny, but she'd meant it seriously.

Happily, Grandfather explained without his having to ask. "What I meant was that it's mostly your inland aunt's husband—that's your great-uncle. He's deaf and dumb. He can't talk except on his fingers, and nobody understands but your little aunt. He can't talk and can't hear, so they don't go visiting. What for?"

Suddenly to be told that he was on his way to a

deaf-mute uncle in a monastery in a marsh was frightening, even with the sun still shining bright. Siebren started to ask about his deaf-and-dumb uncle but pushed it away—it was still too strange; he'd first have to think it out. Instead he asked, "But why do you call my aunt an inland aunt?"

"It's just words," Grandpa said shortly. "It's a little joke between her and me. You've still your Aunt Anna in a village some miles beyond the monastery and the marsh, so she's really more inland. Your little inland aunt is named Hinka. She's my favorite sister, and we were always close. But it's really just words."

He wanted to tell Grandpa they were wonderful words, but he had to ponder because it was almost impossible to think of Grandpa as young and playing with a little sister. Grandpa was old and gray and the chief elder in the church in Weirom, right next to the dominie, who was next to God. His mind hard on that, Siebren heard himself say, "Women don't live in monasteries—women are in convents."

"Smart, aren't you?" Grandpa said severely. "The big farmhouse your aunt lives in was once a real monastery. And I suppose when it was a monastery, it was full of monks—and not a single little aunt."

Taken aback, Siebren stuttered out, "Then is the deaf-and-dumb uncle a monk?"

"Not very smart now," Grandfather said. "You've

stopped using sense. You're just making questions, so let me ask you one. How long ago was the tower in our village built?"

"Much more than a thousand years ago," Siebren said, proud to be prompt after Grandpa had said he was dumb. "In the year eight hundred and forty exactly."

"Well, more or less," Grandpa said. "At least, that's what they say. And they also say that the tower and church of our village were built by those same monks who once lived in the monastery of your inland aunt."

Siebren gasped and gave a startled look to his hand around the cane. He'd squeezed the cane so hard the blood was seeping through the bandage. "Whew," he said aloud. "Whew, I'm going to a house more than a thousand years old that monks once lived in." He whistled sharply to show Grandpa that it wasn't a question—just something exciting he was telling himself.

His whistling didn't do any good. Grandfather looked at him hard and long. "They certainly misnamed you when they called you Siebren," he said. "Your name should have been Mark—Question Mark!"

Siebren laughed to show Grandpa what a good joke that was, then while laughing loudly he dropped ten steps behind. It'd be safer to stay way behind, for then if a question came popping he couldn't possibly ask it without having to shout it. For another safety measure he fixed his eyes on the distant wind-mill. "Dragon—some dragon," he said derisively within himself, and he made a long wry face as if thinking hard about the mill. He wasn't fooling him-self; he was still seething with questions about all the strange things his grandfather had told him.

He eyed the windmill, and now at last he honestly admitted to himself that all the secret games he'd made up about becoming a wayfaring stranger had really been *cheat* games. He wouldn't become a jour-neying stranger until he came to the windmill of Nes. He'd been to the village of Nes before, but just to the church, never as far as the windmill. Why, he'd been to Nes a lot of Sundays.

When Father was home of a Sunday to take care of Knillis, Mother liked to go to the church in Nes. "Just for a change," she'd say. "Just to get you and me, Siebren, out of this eternal house and village."

Mother always said the same thing in the same way every Sunday they went to the church in Nes, and he liked it again every Sunday. It was part of the long walk. When the windmill came into view, Mother would say, "The windmill and I, Siebren—busy, busy, and always busy. But once in a while of a quiet Sunday, the mill and I can fold our wings and come to rest."

That was so nice; it made the whole windmill nice.

"Dragon!" Siebren said aloud. "Some dragon!" he hooted.

Ahead, Grandpa called out, "What did you say? You sound like a rusty old steamboat in a deep fog."

Siebren did not answer but turned away from the windmill to look back at his own distant village. Behind him the dike and the road stretched in long lone emptiness. But beyond Nes, the big windmill began turning slow wings in the evening breeze while Weirom lay back in its sea haze. "Grandpa," he asked anxiously, "my inland aunt, is she nice like my mother?"

"You'll find her fun," Grandpa promptly assured him. "She's old, of course, but she'll have lots of time for you, and small as she is, she'll be more like a play-mate than an aunt. My guess is it'll be about ten thousand times better than sitting with a brother with a sore head."

Now Grandfather was teasing, but it was a nice teasing. The sky in the distance got bright, and it lit up as if with the windmill's turning, the big sweep of the wings were cleaning the sky. Everything suddenly was so much better that Siebren moved close to Grandfather and asked, "Is my great-uncle as small as my inland aunt?"

It was a question, but Grandfather did not seem to mind. "Nope," Grandfather answered. "Quite the opposite. Your great-uncle is a giant—a deaf-mute giant. His name is Siebren too, and he is six feet six! When you see them walking together it's the laughingest sight. He always holds her by the hand, because otherwise she has to scuttle to keep up with him. It's the silliest, laughingest sight—and they're both wonderful."

"Doesn't everybody laugh?" Siebren asked, dismayed.

"Nope," Grandpa said. "In the great swamp where they live, the frogs and storks and cranes and herons don't laugh at them at all."

Oh, it was lovely-wonderful, this thing his stern, serious grandfather had said. And it wasn't a joke; it wasn't teasing. It made it easy to be with Grandpa. Siebren had a bright thought—as bright as the evening sky with the sun going down and the windmill's wings turning. He took his good hand and placed it in Grandfather's hand, and together they walked toward the turning mill. Where the sun went down would be the marsh and the monastery in the marsh, and the frogs and the storks and the cranes and the herons, and two people walking, and nobody laughing, and everything strange, lovely-wonderful.

4

Handball of Satan

It was suppertime in Nes. Only Siebren and Grandfather moved down the long main street. At the far
end, the tall domed windmill stood motionless. No
wings turned; nothing moved. And still in the emptiness there were odd, high-pitched fretting sounds that
seemed to come from behind houses and down side
streets. The sounds could have been the dry squeak-
squeal of the wings of the windmill, but the mill
wasn't turning. It was puzzling. Uneasily, Siebren
hurried after Grandfather.

Soon he lagged again. Nes was a heaven of odors,
and Siebren caught himself sniffing from door to door.

The good sweet odors of frying onions came from behind every door. There was only one odor better than onions frying—fried herring. And this morning Mother had bought a heaping panful of herring— for next to nothing, she'd said. Right now Mother and Knillis would be eating them. Siebren could see the fried fish, golden in the middle of Knillis's high-chair tray, with Mother stooping over it to pick it to boneless morsels. Wonder if there'd be herring at the monastery of the inland aunt?

Siebren started to run after Grandpa to ask him. Grandfather heard him coming. "Yes, come here fast and keep me from temptation. Smell those onions? If that doesn't want to make you break down doors and snatch frying pans off stoves!"

"At home they've got herring," Siebren said sadly.

"Need we bring that up?" Grandpa asked. "You and I walked out of Weirom and away from the biggest, fattest herring of the whole season, and now we have to wade nostril-deep through the onion odors of Nes. . . . Cheer up though, Siebren. Soon we'll be out of it, and then we'll eat our dry, dead sandwiches." Grandpa patted his pocket and laughed.

"We'll get out beyond the windmill and dangle our legs down in a roadside ditch, sit in the grass, and have our banquet of bread. And I deserve prison bread! I walked out of Weirom and never thought to bring my little inland sister a mess of herring. The closest they get to fish is marsh pike and marsh eel, never good saltwater fish."

Siebren had nothing to say, for now he did not need to ask his question about herring at the monastery. He had his answer. In the silence he heard again the high fretting sounds. But now they seemed much closer, and there was an undertone of threat in the shrill keening sounds.

Grandpa too stood half-twisted, listening. "Aha," he said. "The dogs of Nes! I've never known such a village for mean dogs. It's the real reason I brought my cane. We've been saved so far by the onion smells —those dogs are so hungry they're just sitting and keening, so we two strangers have gone unnoticed. But give me my cane; I'm thinking they are gathering and will soon be coming, and I want to be ready. . . . Stay close to me, because I don't think they're going to let us out of Nes without an accounting."

Siebren looked up fearfully, wanting it to be the turning wings of the windmill that made the eerie sounds, but the windmill was still. Now from different points in the village there came sharp, short barks.

Grandfather stopped to listen. "Yes, we've been noticed. They're alerting each other. Strangers in Nes —that's what those high, sharp barks mean, and back of some house or behind some fence they'll be waiting for us. . . . No, keep that thumb up! If you're scared, hang on to my pants with your good hand, because suddenly they'll be around us in one big, cowardly pack, sneaking and curling and winding. But don't get scared and run. Hang on to me, because I'm going to surprise them and wade right into the thick of them with my heavy cane. Quiet now—I think they're behind that next clump of houses."

Siebren glanced fearfully down the long, empty street. He still hadn't seen any dogs, but there was a waiting, skulking silence. He and Grandpa were on the far side of the village now. Up ahead there was an empty space, then the houses began again. Behind the clump of houses rose the windmill.

Grandpa was edging ahead, eyeing the houses. He suddenly pointed. "It'll be from behind that high board fence, I'm betting. . . . Now hang on and wade right in with me. I'm telling you now so you won't be scared when they come."

Scared? He was scared stiff. If Grandpa needed a thick cane. . . . Siebren grabbed blindly with his sore hand, and in spite of the pain, he pinched his grandfather's trouser-leg into a wad for a grip. There wasn't time to do anything else. Suddenly from behind the black fence dogs streamed into the road. The pack came swift, silent—twisting and weaving. It was almost like water flowing around him and Grandpa, then they were surrounded. Pain came stabbing out of Siebren's clutching thumb. In one look he saw blood seeping through the bandage. Then the dogs, silent no more but snarling and snapping, closed in. "Grandpa," Siebren cried, "my thumb's bleeding. What'll they do when they smell blood?"

Grandpa glanced around. "Keep that thumb up! They got around us too fast, so we'll stand still. They're cowards; if we don't move, they won't. But watch the quiet ones—those are the ones to fear—not the yappers. The moment you go for one of the yappers, the quiet ones sneak in and fetch you a mean nab in the leg. Then before you whip around, they're gone a mile. So the idea is to get one of the silent ones first. Make one of *them* yelp, and the yappers are all done. You watch—one crack, one yelp, and the whole pack will have melted away. . . . All right, I've picked my dog to wallop; now hang on." Even as he said it, Grandpa, without taking the cane from his shoulder, twisted on his heels and took one giant stride into the dog pack. He ripped loose from Siebren's hold, and Siebren stood alone. The near dogs, startled, set themselves in new, stiff positions. Again Grandpa stepped out, but he stumbled and lurched forward. He almost fell, but at the last moment he struck out with the cane. With a sickening thud the cane lashed across the pack and came down on the hunched-up, bony back of a small dog on the far outside. The little dog yelped and leaped high.

Yelping, yipping, shrilling, the scared, hurt dog plunged through the pack, whip-tailing himself down

the road toward the windmill. The dog ran on three legs, its one hind leg drawn up high and tight and pained into the hollow flank of its thin little body. The three-legged speed of the sorry, skinny dog was amazing. It ran on and on in shrill misery. It ran alone. The pack had melted, vanished. Siebren and Grandpa stood alone.

"Hey, I didn't mean to hit *him*," Grandpa said regretfully. "I stumbled and then hit that poor worm—is he going to the mill? That's all I need—for him to belong to the miller of Nes. . . ." Then Grandfather looked at Siebren. "Thumb all right?" He noticed Siebren's look. "Don't you stand there looking at me like that," he said severely. "I stumbled, and the cane came down on his back. You don't actually think I'd hit a crippled dog, do you? Now stop! You'd think I had hit you."

"He keeps sounding so awful," Siebren said woefully.

Then the nearby windmill began turning in a late gust of evening wind, and the slow, dry squealings of its great wings mixed oddly with the yippings of the little dog. When the dog got behind the mill he was still. Moments later the big wings of the mill stopped.

"It's getting dark," Grandpa said, "and the way that pack of dogs left so suddenly, I wouldn't be surprised they'll be back in the dark. Let's get away from Nes as fast as we can. With my good cane I don't mind fighting them again, but I don't see so well in the dark."

Grandfather didn't return the cane but strode up the road so fast Siebren had to trot to keep up. He worriedly touched the seeping bandage as he ran. Behind Grandpa he wormed and twisted the bandaged hand into his pocket. Thin stringy tinglings ran from his spine up his neck at the thought of the dog pack coming up behind him in the gathering dark. They wouldn't need to see—dogs could smell blood for miles. His thumb would give them away, and Grandpa couldn't see in the dark.

There was no sound but their own hurrying feet. There was nothing behind them, nothing sneaking along among the clumps of roadside bushes. Even the three-legged dog had disappeared. The great windmill loomed above them, and it was as if the night's darkness was gathering around the rounded dome—as if the mill were pulling down the darkness.

Then out of the dark dome—sudden as a thunderclap a loud voice said, "Good evening, young wayfaring stranger down the road. Wherever the trip leads you, may it fare you well. It will bring you good things. Only believe it."

Startled, Siebren and Grandfather stopped. They stared up at the dark mill. There, almost hidden by an upright wing, a head poked out of a little oval window so small that its frame seemed to fit around the neck of the poking head. It was startling, but it wasn't scary—it was as if the voice coming down from the sky had swept all the fear of the dog pack away. Siebren murmured: "Wayfaring stranger." He sighed with delight. It was much better than journeying stranger. He tasted the words the whole length of his tongue.

Then Grandfather said the words too, but he grunted them. "Wayfaring stranger," he snorted. "Wayfaring stranger, indeed!" He suddenly grabbed Siebren by the arm, tugged the sore hand out of the pocket without seeing it, and pulled Siebren on down the road. "Wayfaring stranger," Grandpa said in disgust. "When he knows me as well as I know my own goats and chickens. Don't we go to the same church? Don't I as elder stand before him every Sunday, reading the lesson? Wayfaring stranger! But odd men, odd deeds—and also odd words, I guess."

Siebren was tugged along unwillingly. "But Grandpa, he meant me! He said *young* wayfaring stranger."

"Oh, so!" Grandpa let go of Siebren to look back at the mill. "So now the miller of Nes makes a point of ignoring me by greeting you."

Siebren stared up at Grandfather, bewildered. Grandpa had not liked it when he'd thought the miller had called *him* a wayfaring stranger, but now he didn't like it that the miller *hadn't* called him a wayfaring stranger. Mother and all the women of Peppermint Street didn't like the miller of Nes either. And still the miller had called down such wonderful things in wonderful words. It was like a song, like a psalm out of the Bible: "Wayfaring stranger—may the trip fare you well. It will bring you good things. Only believe it."

The words stayed sounding wonderful, but now they were like treason within him—treason to Mother and to Grandfather. Way back in Weirom he had decided that the trip was magic, and now the miller of Nes had made it magic. "It will bring you good things. Only believe it." Siebren touched the flat tin in his pocket for good luck. "Why don't you like the miller of Nes, Grandpa?" he asked softly as he jogged beside the striding old man.

Grandpa grumped and cleared his throat. "He's pretty small, if you ask me," Grandpa said. "Pretty small! Charged me seventeen cents too much for a bag of chicken feed but would never admit it. That was over a year ago, and of course we don't speak, even if we are from the same church. I don't buy from him anymore. An odd man, I say, always doing odd things, and thinking and talking in odd ways, like nobody else. If you ask me, the miller of Nes is a handball of Satan."

Grandpa said it in a hard, round voice as if reading it while standing before the congregation on Sunday.

"Why, Grandpa—because he says odd things like that about wayfaring stranger?" Siebren asked. "Why is he a handball of Satan? What does it mean?"

Grandfather didn't even hear. "Pretty small," he fumed. "A whole year of anger over seventeen cents. But that's what happens when you let yourself become a handball of Satan."

Grandpa hurled himself down the road in long strides, his cane striking sparks out of the flint stones in the gravel. There were tiny, thin smells of sulphur. "A handball of Satan," Grandpa said behind clenched teeth, "for Satan to play with." A wind began to blow in the dark. Behind them the wings of the windmill began to squeal out in dry, lonely pain, as if they had been hurt like the bone-skinny dog.

"From the same church," Grandpa spoke out again, following his angry thoughts. He struck the gravel. Siebren's side began to ache from trotting so hard to keep up. His thumb hurt. He held his sore hand against his sore side. "A whole year, Siebren," Grandpa said loudly. "A whole year and not one word—for seventeen cents." Grandpa stopped and looked down at Siebren.

"You either?" Siebren blurted out, amazed that anyone could be still a whole entire year.

"Of course not," Grandpa said indignantly. He looked hard at Siebren. "What did you say?"

He'd just blurted it out because his thumb hurt and his side ached; now it scared him—what he'd dared to say. Now he'd have to repeat it. Desperately he searched his mind for something else. Then like a flash it came. For safety he backed off a little. "Well, when I fight with Knillis, Mother says if I want to fight with him it's all right, but then I have to make myself as small as he is. But since I can't do that, why don't I just make myself bigger by not fighting with little Knillis?"

To Siebren's surprise, Grandfather asked with a slow smile, "Yes, and what then?"

"Then I guess that makes me feel so big I don't want to fight. Mother says that to fight you have to be small."

Grandpa held out his cane as if he were going to strike with it, but he only said, "My daughter says that?"

Siebren nodded, scared.

Slowly, solemnly, Grandpa said, "Siebren, you help me remember, will you, that when we get home, I have to have my daughter take me over her knee and give me a good hard spanking? So you have to be small to fight? Well then, I've been pretty small for a whole year over seventeen cents. Remember too that I owe *you* seventeen cents for telling me what my daughter says about fighting. So now I'm marching myself back to that miller to make up with him and to give him his seventeen cents."

Siebren was so startled that he just stood looking.

Grandpa turned and started for the mill. Siebren started after him.

"No, Siebren. This we have to settle by ourselves. You stay here. . . . Say, why don't you sit down by this ditch and eat your sandwiches?"

"But you said that whole pack of dogs might come back after dark—and it's dark, and you've got the cane."

Grandpa looked down the dark road toward the village. "They won't come now anymore," he decided. "But here—here's my cane. Oh, here is your seventeen cents too. That ought to make you feel better. I'll be back in minutes."

It seemed Grandfather had to do this right now, this minute. He walked away fast. Siebren was left standing in the road, scared and forlorn, but he held the seventeen cents clutched in his good hand. Seventeen cents! And Grandpa hadn't been angry—he'd been thankful.

In the glow of the seventeen cents, he obeyed his grandfather. He went to the roadside ditch and sat, legs hanging over the water, and one by one he let the coins slide deep in his pants pocket. It took time, but that way he didn't think of the dogs and the dark and the stillness. Hey, already it was coming out as the miller said—good things. He sat in such a way that his pants stretched tight over the money in his pocket. It was as if he could feel each coin and tell them apart by the feel. One nickel, seven pennies, and ten halfpennies. There they lay. He counted the felt but unseen coins over and over. Then he thought a crazy thing—wouldn't it be nice to have a tiny pouch in your skin the way kangaroos in Australia had pouches? Oh, just a small one, just big enough for seventeen cents. He giggled. But it sounded loud in the stillness.

He'd better eat his sandwiches—Grandfather had said to. A stab of doubt passed through him. Often big people just told kids anything to get rid of them— they just said the first thing. In the village Grandpa had said the dogs would come back, but when he wanted to go back to the miller, he said the dogs wouldn't come back. Siebren laid the cane across his knees in readiness, reached back, and touched the tin in his pocket for luck. If only Mother hadn't stamped it flat, wouldn't it have been a fine, lucky place to keep the seventeen cents?

The water in the ditch just below his dangling feet stood still; everything stood still. He dug the sandwiches out of his pocket with his good hand. Dogs could jump ditches! He'd never see them coming be- cause of the bushes. Suddenly the whole pack would come sailing over the ditch. He laid his sore hand on the cane. He'd eat fast with his good hand and get rid of the food smell—dogs smell things for miles.

Down the road the windmill began to squeak—slow,

mournful, lone. Then it sounded as if the whole mill were stamping down the road. But still, it was more the sound of something falling hard down many stairs. Grandpa was there alone with the miller of Nes, who handled big horses. Grandpa was old. The miller was a handball of Satan, and maybe he'd thrown Grandpa down all the narrow stairways of all the lofts in the mill—all the way from the high oval window down to the door. There Grandpa lay. He wouldn't come; he wouldn't ever come, but the dog pack of Nes would come.

He tried to make his scared mind blank. The windmill had stopped its squealing and pounding. Now everything was still again.

Siebren stared over the ditch. Something was staring back at him! Two eyes reflected red from the little light on the water. Siebren sat rigid, not daring to stir. Then with one hand he fumbled at the sandwich package to shut out the food smell, his sore hand clamped around the cane. The eyes were still there.

Whatever it was moved and went down into the deep grass. Something black came squeezing through the grass to the very edge of the ditch opposite him. It was a dog! It was the little black dog Grandpa had hit with his cane, coming for him. Siebren knuckled both hands around the thick cane. Then at the very edge of the ditch the little dog raised up on his hind legs, begging for food, his little forepaws hanging. It had come to the sandwich smell. It only wanted food. Siebren hid the cane behind him and opened the package of sandwiches.

The begging dog had sat up on his sore hind leg too long; suddenly he pitched forward and fell head-long into the ditch. There was a great noisy splash; water washed up around Siebren's shoes, sprayed up, and showered down on his Sunday suit. The little dog had gone down—he stayed down horrible long moments. But then there was a welling and a bubbling at Siebren's feet, and up came the shaggy black head. The little dog had swum to him underwater. He could swim with three legs, but he couldn't climb the steep bank with only three. He splashed and splashed his paws until he could plant them on Siebren's feet. The moment he pulled his head up out of water he lifted his little begging nose to the sandwich smell—he was so dreadfully hungry.

Siebren broke off a piece of bread and dropped it. The little dog snapped the bread out of the air so hard his teeth clicked. That was a little scary, but since the dog's mouth was full of bread, Siebren threw himself flat, reached down, and pulled the little dog out of the water by his front paws—they weren't sore.

The wet dog didn't shake himself or wag his tail; he went straight to the sandwiches. He gulped the three sandwiches whole in three wrenching swallows. Then he looked up and wagged his tail, shook himself, and sprayed Siebren with a fine spray of water. Siebren said, "That's my Sunday suit, you!" At Siebren's voice the little dog began wagging his tail so hard it sounded like hissing snakes in the tall grass. Siebren reached out and patted him on his head. Then they talked. Siebren talked little soft friendly words, and the dog talked with his tail in the swishing grass. And then— well, they were friends. Such friends that Siebren dared to take hold of the drawn-up, sore leg. The dog watched Siebren's hand, but he didn't growl or snap; he just watched. Siebren remembered the extra cloths for bandages Mother had shoved into his pocket. He pulled them out. "Look," he said, "for almost no good reason Mother put these in my pocket. The miller of Nes said the trip was going to bring many good things —see, now it's brought bandages for you."

He took gently hold of the little leg. "I know how to bandage," he told the dog. "I watched my mother. Look, I've got a sore thumb; you've got a sore leg. A good tight bandage helps. I know from my thumb." It wasn't as easy as he'd thought because his wrapped thumb got in the way. "Now don't you mind," he cautioned. "I have to do it tight. Else it won't help."

The little dog found Grandpa's cane in the grass and kept sniffing it while the slow bandaging was going on. Maybe he remembered the cane because he stood very still and obedient while Siebren fumbled with the bandage. It was hard work, and it took a long time, but nobody cared because when at last it was done, the leg was straight and not drawn up into the ribby little body. The little dog put his paw down on the ground and sniffed at the bandage. Then he looked up and wagged his tail.

Siebren was triumphant. The white bandage looked important and healing around the dog's leg. They'd been strangers, but now they trusted each other. Why, they were both wayfaring strangers. Siebren told the dog about it. "You know what I'd call you if you were mine? Wayfarer!" He sighed. Oh, the little dog ought to be fat and shiny and full of fun—and have a name and be his—his dog! Just his.

Down the road, gravel crunched and Grandfather came hurrying. Like a wisp—as if nothing had ever been—the little dog was gone. Unseen, belly low in the grass, he sneaked away, and only Siebren knew because where the grass was flattened, the white bandage showed.

Then Grandfather was there. "Well, I see you ate your sandwiches. Looks as if you chewed the paper too—were you that hungry? . . . Well, I'd better munch mine as we march along. Going back to that mill held us up quite a bit. But it was worth it—we talked everything out. I even tried to help the miller with his mill —some big wooden cog had slipped; that's why it was so noisy. Guess you could hear it way out here."

Grandfather seemed very pleased with himself. Uneasy about the little dog, Siebren did not know what to say. Boy, was he going to be hungry with Grandpa munching away! Grandpa seemed to be waiting for him to say something, so for a little joke he said, "Won't Mother have to take you over her knees and give you that spanking now?"

"Guess not," Grandpa said. "Disappointing, no? But I guess I don't need that spanking now. Broke three fingernails helping that miller . . . that's a good enough deed for any day—when it breaks off your fingernails."

He and Grandpa laughed together. Hey, now he and Grandpa were *wayfaring* friends! They *were* friends, because all of a sudden Grandpa said: "Here, since all boys are bottomless pits," and handed him the biggest half of his sandwich. That meant there'd be more coming, for Mother had given Grandpa three sandwiches too. It was another good thing! The miller had said, "May it bring you good things—only believe it." He believed it.

Oh, it was close and chummy with Grandpa now, munching away together down the dark road. He was carrying Grandpa's cane for his sore thumb, but Wayfarer was wearing his bandages. Wayfarer was full of his sandwiches, but he, Siebren, was eating Grandpa's sandwiches, and nobody was hungry anymore—nobody needed bandages. Nobody. Nobody at all.

5

New Store and New School

All the way from the windmill of Nes to the next village of Lahsens, Siebren kept watching the hedges and ditch banks for a sign of the little dog. Somewhere in the dark, keeping out of sight in the tall grass and behind bushes, Wayfarer might be following them.

Oh, he must be! He wasn't to be seen because he was afraid of Grandpa, who'd hit him with the cane. Siebren thought indignantly about Grandpa and his cane, but that was because he had been tricking Grandpa all the way from the windmill.

He began whistling his tuneless song again, but he was really whistling to let the little dog know where he was. Bit by bit he whistled louder and louder so that it would go back to Nes and to Wayfarer.

Then Grandfather turned around and stopped all whistling. "Siebren, if possible, you're even worse than your mother. She couldn't whistle either when she was a kid. But you sound like nothing but a frog in a fog."

Grandpa had called Mother a kid! Siebren was too surprised to be hurt at what Grandfather had said about his whistling. But now he'd better think up some other trick for letting Wayfarer know where he was. He dropped behind so he'd have to talk loudly. "Wayfarer," he called out. "Grandpa, isn't that a wonderful word—WAYFARER?"

Grandfather had enough of that immediately. He waited for Siebren to trot up. "What's all this way-farer business and this shouting? I haven't suddenly gone deaf."

Hey, now he had even Grandfather saying Way-farer! And if the little dog heard Grandfather using his name, maybe he wouldn't be so scared any more and would really follow.

It smote him. His whole trick was for nothing. He'd given the dog the name, and he'd spoken it once, but the little dog hadn't *learned* his name was Wayfarer. He wouldn't come if you said it a thousand times. He didn't know it. Siebren made a face at himself and sighed at his own foolishness. "Grandpa," he said in a low, dull voice. "Did you ever have a dog?"

"Nope. Never liked them," Grandpa promptly answered.

Siebren walked on behind, silent and heavy. It was as if a door had slammed shut in a high wind. It made him feel cold and shut out. He thought about his mother being a kid, not able to whistle either, and he began to make play-talk with her so he wouldn't feel so empty and lonely and faraway.

"Mother?" he said. "Mother, if I take good care of Knillis all the time every day, could I have this little dog?"

"All the time?" Mother asked him in his mind.

He made believe he misunderstood. "Yes, all the time," he answered her. "Every day after school and all day Saturday—even Sundays if you want to go to church at Nes with Father."

"No, I meant," Mother corrected, "keep a dirty skinny crippled dog here all the time? To the end of all our days?"

The words—to the end of all our days—had just come from nowhere. Oh, he liked them!

He hurried to tell Mother in his mind, "Not dirty and skinny and crippled, Mother! I'll wash him and feed him and fix his leg up. His name is Wayfarer. And there he will be—to the end of all our days."

"To the end of all our days," he said aloud and listened to the longing in the sound. All of a sudden he felt himself become a bundle of trembly longing.

Instead of going on with Grandpa to the monastery, he wanted to go home.

On the way back he'd find Wayfarer. Grandpa would go on, but he'd run back. Then as he got far from Grandpa, there from behind a black bush would show a white bandage, and Wayfarer would come wagging to him.

They'd go home together. Long before Nes he would pick up Wayfarer and throw him over his shoulders like a newborn lamb. Holding Wayfarer by his four legs, he'd be wearing him like a scarf. That's the way he'd carry him around Nes and its mean, miserable curs. Wayfarer wouldn't leave any ground scent then for the dog pack to pick up and trail, and they'd both be safe. Dark as it was, they'd both be safe.

Soon they'd stand at the closed door of his own house, and he'd knock in the night. Mother would come in her nightgown, open the upper half of the door a little crack, and peer out scared and doubtful. But then she'd see it was he, wearing Wayfarer around his neck. "Mother," he'd say, "I've come back."

In his mind Siebren hastily changed his inside talk to more careful words: "Mother, I couldn't be away from you and Knillis—not all night and everything. I've come back. Grandpa said this poor dog needs a home."

Siebren listened to himself and nodded. That made it sound as if Grandpa had told him to go back home

—almost as if Grandfather had *ordered* him to bring the little dog home. What then if Mother should open the door wide and say: "Of course, we'll keep your Wayfarer—we'll keep him to the end of all our days."

He listened to the words he'd made Mother say in his mind, and he was deeply moved. "To the end of all our days," he mumbled aloud. It sounded like a prayer; it was as lovely as a litany. Lovely, longing words like that—Mother couldn't possibly refuse him!

He heard his own broken mumble and glanced fearfully toward his grandfather to see if he had heard. Grandfather would think it odd, his talking out loud to himself. That's what Grandfather had said about the miller of Nes: "Odd man, odd talk, but then he's a handball of Satan."

Oh, it was dark here—not a light in any window. But in the black dark he'd been making talk back and forth to Mother. But he often talked and thought odd things inside his mind, and playacted, and *did* odd things when there was nobody to watch him. Did that mean—would that mean he was a handball of Satan too?

It didn't mean that you were a big black ball that Satan had put you in to bounce you around, the way he'd thought it was with the miller of Nes. It must mean that Satan made you do anything he wanted— the way you made a rubber ball do what you wanted by bouncing it around.

It must be that way. It *must* be Satan. Here Grandfather was taking him on the most wonderful trip of his life, and here he'd wanted to run home. He blushed in the dark at the shamefulness of what he'd just played out in his mind. What if instead he'd just said right out to Grandpa: "I don't want to go. I'm going back home and find that dog you hit. Anyway, I'm afraid of a big deaf-and-dumb uncle in a big black marsh."

He walked aghast. Imagine him saying that. He anxiously looked up the road where Grandpa must be. "Grandpa!" he yelled.

Grandfather turned, and Siebren saw the white of his face come out from the somber black of his clothes. He had to say something after yelling like that. "Grandpa," he said, "that little dog you hit by mistake, does he have a home? You said he maybe belonged to the miller of Nes. Did he?"

"No, he didn't—but are you still busy with that two-cent worm of a dog?" Grandpa asked, amazed. "I was wondering why you were dragging. I thought maybe you were sorry you'd come. I had it figured you were going to let me go on alone into that marsh."

"Oh no, Grandpa," Siebren gasped out. Grandpa had come so close it was as if he'd seen into his mind. But Grandfather knew about people who were handballs of Satan and thought odd, and who said and did odd things. "Grandpa," he said, tumbling out the words, "did we pass Lahsens in the dark? Are we at the marsh?"

"Now that was an odd thing to ask," Grandfather said severely. "Have we come through any village streets? What in blazes have you been up to—cane on the wrong shoulder, sore hand rammed down in your pocket? What have you been doing?"

"Nothing." Siebren hastily changed the cane and stood confused. "I guess I'm tired," he said. "Will we be in Lahsens soon? I don't see lights."

"We're all but standing in Lahsens," Grandpa said. "I guess I can't blame you for thinking we were already at the marsh. That's Lahsens for you—black as a moor. They sit in the dark in their houses in the evening and call it 'dusking.' It's a custom here in this miserly village—it saves oil. Why, they don't let their lamplighter light the street lamps until he can hardly find them. Even then he'd better be mighty sure it's going to stay dark all night. You see, the moon might come out, and moonlight's cheaper than kerosene."

It was a joke of course. It was good to hear a joke. It meant Grandpa hadn't been too terribly disappointed when he'd thought that he had wanted to run home.

"Well, if there doesn't come the lamplighter now," Grandpa said. "They must have heard us, and just to put us in our place, they're going to light up the streets of Lahsens."

Up ahead in the black, a dim man with a high,

flickery flame at the top of a pole began stringing the streetlights out before them as he went from lamp to lamp. It was almost as if he were spreading a long line of Christmas welcome-lights out ahead of them. Golden pools of light shone down from the lamps and lay in the street. It was as if Lahsens met them with friendly light.

In the long street, Grandpa and Siebren walked from pool to pool of light until there were no more streetlamps and the black began again. Then beyond the darkness at the far end of the street there still was one lone light. But it came from a big square window.

Grandpa pointed. "See that window? I wouldn't be surprised but that's the new store of my old friend Freerk, the dike inspector. He's too new to Lahsens yet; he doesn't know about dusking; he just wastes oil and has light.

"Remember Freerk in his high hat going along the top of the dike, inspecting both sides of it? Oh, you must remember—he didn't quit that long ago, did he? No matter how bad the storm, Freerk always came through, and no sea wind blew that could blow off his hat. . . . Well anyway now, high hat and all, he's retired from babying the dike and has a little store. He's an elder too—but here in the church in Lahsens now. When he was still dike inspector, he used to stop, and we'd talk church things, but now we haven't had any good church talk in over a year."

Grandpa sounded excited, and he sounded wistful.

"Yes," he said suddenly, "that's what we'll do. We'll stop in for a rest—you said you were tired." Grandfather made a little choked laugh of a sound. "Imagine old Freerk now a storekeeper! Toys and notions—of all things. Thread and rickrack and ribbon and stuff like that. But I bet he wears his high hat to sell it."

"*Toys?*" Siebren asked eagerly. He looked down the dark street to the big bright window. The light showed two high piles of rubble heaped up in front of the store. But this side of the window the whole block was dark from the high walls of a boarded-up building.

Hey, but if they were going into the toystore, he could watch for Wayfarer! So much light shone from the window it fell across the whole street and ranged up the wall of the house opposite the store. Wayfarer had only three good legs, so he might be way behind. What if he'd really come, and the white bandage would show out of the dark as Wayfarer limped into the light from the window?

What a wonderful way—look out of a toystore and find Wayfarer!

Inside himself Siebren prayed: "Make it happen. Lord, make it happen, amen." He rattled it fast because Grandpa was looking at him. He'd prayed with his cap on, so maybe it wouldn't count. No, a prayer with your cap on could hardly count—but Grandpa had been looking.

To prevent any questions he asked, "Grandpa, what is the big building? It's so dark."

"Didn't you know?" Grandpa was surprised. "That's the new Lahsens school. It's your father that's building it."

"Way out here?" he asked, unbelieving. It seemed as if he were almost out of the world, yet here he stood before a school his father was building. Father had been here all day, now he—Siebren—was here, and his father was home with Mother and Knillis. It could be—Father had just got a new bicycle, a swift English three-speed one. "I didn't know it was here my father was building the school," he said.

"It's because you don't listen," Grandfather said. "Your father's remodeling the dike inspector's store too. But that's just a little job, as a favor to an old friend of mine. He's remodeling the store himself while his crew works on the school. That way he can keep an eye on everything."

"My father?" It was overwhelming. He stared at the big building. "But why is it all boarded up—even the big front door and all the windows?"

"They have to do that every night to keep the Lahsens kids from wrecking it—and maybe breaking their silly necks . . . but come on!"

With Grandfather, Siebren walked between the two piles of rubble left from Father's work. Then Grandpa threw open the door without even knocking! But then that was right—it was a store.

As the door flew open a bell rang, and a surprised man jumped out of an armchair, then saw it was

81

Grandpa and came with hands outstretched. They both began talking and laughing and shaking hands. The dike inspector didn't even notice Siebren and his bandaged thumb as he stood in the door with his cane. The inspector wasn't wearing a high hat as Grandpa had said. Siebren was disappointed. But the inspector did have a very bald head—the bright lamplight bounced from it.

Then suddenly the man said, "Sonny, I don't know of anything worse in a store than a boy with a cane on his shoulder, except maybe a bull with six pairs of horns on his head." Still talking and talking to Grandpa, he took the cane away from Siebren, shoved the door shut, dimmed the lamp in this end of the store, and sat down in front of Grandpa.

Siebren felt strange standing, cap politely in hand, against the closed door. He was disappointed in the whole store—even though his father was making it. Except for the big window, it looked almost more like a living room than a store. Why, the far wall beyond the big window still had two closet beds in it. And before the partly closed door of one bed stood a table and chairs. On the table were teacups and a teapot under a cozy. Right in the middle of all that stood a heaping big plate of cookies.

Suddenly the dike inspector turned to Siebren and said, "Sonny, go watch the goldfish in the big window —they're kissing goldfish. If you make kissing sounds above their water, they'll come up and kiss and nibble your lips."

"They do?" Siebren asked. He didn't care about the old goldfish—the man just didn't want him to be a bother. Well, he'd go make believe he was watching the goldfish, but instead he'd really be watching for Wayfarer through the big window. At the window the goldfish came up, pushed their mouths out of the water, and made small clabbering sounds at him.

It startled Siebren. The sounds were almost like the sounds of a small dog's padding feet. Of course, you couldn't really hear the sounds of a dog's feet—not through a window! It was only a hope-sound that your mind made up because you wanted so badly to have Wayfarer come.

Nothing came. Nothing moved—only the goldfish. Siebren glanced around the living-room part of the store. It didn't even look like a store! Grandfather had said toys. There were no toys in this part of the room, nothing but new shelves with boxes. There was one little showcase in the dim end of the room where the men sat, but it was mostly hidden by the two hard-talking old men and their chairs.

Guilty because he'd looked around the store instead of watching the street, Siebren leaned over the goldfish bowl again. The lighted street lay empty. Nothing had come. Suddenly he couldn't stand the clabbery sounds from the silly, stupid round-mouthed

goldfish one moment more. That's all they could do—
clabber in their thick milky water, and the water
smelled; it made his stomach roil. He hastily sat down
in the nearest chair so he wouldn't be above the goldfish bowl, then noticed it was a fancy velvet chair. He
tried to sit very innocent, a polite question already
formed in his mouth in case the bald man looked up:
"Is it all right if I sit in this chair?"

Nobody looked up, but Siebren sat uneasy. It was
a fancy, soft, green velvet chair—it wasn't for boys.

He looked at the table below the doors of the closet
beds. What a heap of cookies for just two people—
he didn't even know if the dike inspector had a wife
—Grandpa hadn't said. But there were two tea cups
and two chairs. It sure was a lot of cookies. What if
Wayfarer should still come? What could he do about
Wayfarer in the street?

Siebren's mind raced. He'd quick say to Grandpa,
"Oh Grandpa, there's that little dog you hit by mistake. He followed us." While he was saying it he'd
hurry to the door, open it a crack, and throw out some
cookies to little Wayfarer.

Most likely the two old men would never notice.
But Wayfarer would smell the cookies and know that
he—Siebren—was inside and wait for more cookies.

Eyes on the two men, heart pounding, Siebren
sidled over to the table below the closet-bed doors.
As he bent down to sit his hand snake-darted out

and grabbed. In one breathless motion he shoved a whole handful of cookies down in his jacket pocket. The old men had gone on talking, but above the table that door of the one closet bed—was it more open? Was somebody in the bed?

Siebren bolted to the window. The deed was done, but his heart was pounding so hard that even his sore thumb thumped and throbbed. He plumped down in the velvet chair.

Uneasily he looked over his shoulder. A bed door partly open usually meant somebody was in the closet bed because the door had to be open for air. What if they'd watched him stealing cookies?

The thought made him feel even more guilty about sitting in the velvet chair. He'd pulled Wayfarer out of the water; Wayfarer had sprayed water all over him—what if he was still damp and had left a stain on the green velvet seat? They'd even think it was because he didn't know enough to ask to go to the bathroom.

Siebren pushed a wary hand under himself. Thank goodness, there wasn't even a touch of dampness. He looked down at himself and gasped. He wasn't buttoned! It gaped! Grandpa hadn't buttoned him all up—two buttons in a row were loose. What if it was a woman in the bed behind the partly opened door? If it was a boy, you could just say something easy like "Two o'clock in the button factory," and laugh and button up, but what if it was a woman? He sat rigid with shame. Desperately he fumbled at the buttons and knew he was helpless. He couldn't button with one hand! Oh, now he'd fumbled another button loose—three buttons in a row. Now his underwear even showed. He sagged in shame.

He tried to button himself with his sore hand. It hurt. His thumb throbbed from his clumsy fumblings. The thick bunched bandage got in his way. But thick as it was, blood began seeping through. Now what if he dripped blood on the green velvet chair. It would show a mile.

"I can't, I can't," he whimpered. He heard himself and jumped out of the chair. Thank goodness he didn't gape when he stood up tall and straight. He took a deep breath and eyed the closet bed. No, the door hadn't opened one bit more. It must be there wasn't anyone in the bed after all. He looked toward Grandfather. "Grandpa, will you button me—I can't." He tried the words, mouthed them, and took a doubtful step toward the old men. He whirled at a small running sound right behind him. It was only the miserable goldfish clabbering at the top of the water again. He glanced toward the window.

THERE—there in the light in the street sat Wayfarer! There he sat, his sharp nose sniffing. Wayfarer had found him! Wayfarer!

Siebren didn't have to think what to do because he was doing it. He rushed to the door, opened it, and called over his shoulder, "Grandpa, I'm going to look at Father's new school."

Outside the door he listened. No chair scraped. Nobody came out of the house. But out of the pool of light Wayfarer came to him, and already he had his sharp nose up to the cookies in Siebren's pocket. Siebren didn't give him a single cookie. Suddenly he knew what to do.

He ran with Wayfarer to the new school, searched and found the blade of an old broken spade, and with it pried and worked one side of the boarded door off its nails, pulled it out, shoved Wayfarer through, and tossed all the cookies in after him. He could hear Wayfarer crunching cookies. He hammered the plank door back on its nails.

It was as if everything went of itself, and now it was done. Grandpa had said, "If everything's well in the morning, sometime that same day Siebren and I will come stamping home again." On their way back he'd let Wayfarer out and take him home!

The thought smote him—what if everything didn't go well, and they didn't come by tomorrow—what then? Then—as if of itself—it became clear just what to do. He'd run through a pile of trash somebody had burned in the front yard of the school; he'd kick up all kinds of charred sticks; they'd be swell to write with. He gathered a handful and hurried back to the door.

He wrote in big clumsy letters over the whole door:

DAD. THE DOG IS WAYFARER. I FOUND HIM AND BANDAGED HIM. IF I TAKE CARE OF KNILLIS, CAN'T I TAKE CARE OF WAYFARER TOO? MAYN'T I HAVE HIM, DAD?

It took time, but then it was done. Siebren looked toward the store window, looked back at his sign, and in the one clear space left on the door wrote the biggest words of all:

PLEASE, DAD.

There it stood, big and black—please—it begged Dad.

Father couldn't help seeing it when he forced the door open in the morning. But now he had to get back to the store or he'd be missed. Siebren rubbed his smudged hand down his trouser leg before he remembered it was his Sunday suit, then ran for the store.

6

The Woman in the Bed

Siebren ran so fast that he didn't slow down nearly enough as he dashed back to the store. He burst through the door and slammed it shut behind him. The slam shook the house. The oil lamp shivered. The two old men, startled out of their talk, stared mutely.

"A big dog came after me," Siebren mumbled to Grandpa.

It wasn't heard. The two old men, after peering at him without understanding, leaned forward in their chairs, picked up their words and talked again.

Relieved, Siebren pushed past them to go back to

the lighted living-room part of the store. He stopped, mouth open. There in the high closet bed sat a woman. She'd thrown the bed door wide open, and there she sat, big arms crossed over her nightgown, blinking and looking at him. "Oh, you scared me with that door," she said. "I'd gone to bed early with a headache. Then when you two came in, I had to keep so mouse-quiet I guess I fell asleep."

Siebren couldn't utter a sound; he could only stand stupid, staring. His face flamed as he remembered the cookies and the buttons. He helplessly hoped the woman didn't know—that she'd been asleep as she said.

Now the woman grinned. "Look sonny, don't just stand there—you can help both of us out. I want to get up and get dressed, but I can't with those two sitting there. But see those drapes bunched up against the wall? Well, they're to divide our living room from the store part. So if you'll pull them across for me, then you can go right on through that hall door to the bathroom. Meanwhile, I'll get dressed, and in that way you and I can get buttoned and proper at the same time."

She smiled such a nice reassuring smile Siebren fairly leaped for the drapes. She knew about the buttons, so she knew about the cookies too, but she was all smiley and nice. She was nice—she'd even joked. She was easy-funny. He struggled the drapes across the room, but he had to poke his head through a

91

moment and tell her, "I'll be right back—all buttoned up." He ran down the hall, letting his grateful laughter run out behind him to show her all his love and gratitude. Why, if he told her about Wayfarer, she wouldn't even care about the cookies—not if they were for Wayfarer. She was good.

In the little bathroom, he sagged a moment in enormous relief, then reached for the buttons. In his grateful relief at her niceness, he'd completely forgotten he couldn't button buttons. Alone here, secret and private, he tried fiercely and desperately. It was impossible. All he did was make his thumb bleed. A big drop of blood plopped from the tip of the bandage to the white bathroom floor. He rubbed it out with the toe of his shoe—what if that had happened on the velvet chair! He stood biting his lip. In total defeat he dribbled back to the store part of the living room.

The drapes were still drawn across the room; the woman was behind them. Siebren eyed the men, trying to get up courage to interrupt and softly ask Grandpa to button him. He coughed. Coughed again —hard, so that he had to hold his stomach. If Grandpa looked, he might see that he was unbuttoned. He circled behind the men's chairs so that he could lean over Grandpa's shoulder and whisper to him. Then he stopped. Hidden by the two old men and their chairs, the little showcase he'd seen from the big window was absolutely jammed full of rubber balls!

The balls had been built into a pyramid the way he built blocks for Knillis. Blocks were square, but these were round balls in a pyramid! Of course, the ends of the showcase helped hold them up, but at the bottom —right in the middle, acting as foundation for the pyramid—was the biggest ball he had ever seen. It was black—shiny black—it even shone in this dim end of the room.

Oh, *it* was the handball of Satan! That's what he would name it—Satan. Yes, Satan. Look at it! Why, if he were to come home with a ball like that, none of the kids of Weirom would believe it.

Behind the old men, Siebren laughed a silent delighted laugh. Why, in all the history of Weirom, even from the time the monks built the tower, there'd never been a ball like that. Imagine him coming home with it. The kids would come right out and beg: "Can we play with your ball, Siebren? Can't we play with it while you have to sit with Knillis? You can't lose a big ball like that!"

He'd just say, "No, you can't play with Satan." That would scare the kids all right.

He moved toward the ball in the showcase as if it pulled him. All his thoughts went leaping—imagine if on the biggest journey of your life you got the biggest ball in the whole world. . . . He'd be sitting with Knillis, but all the kids would be hanging around in Peppermint Street, and every once in a while one of them would come to the window and yell, "Can't we just play with it until you come out? Can't you ever come out?"

He'd shake his head and build up blocks for Knillis. The ball would lie beside the high chair. Immediately he changed the picture—the ball was beside Wayfarer. Wayfarer lay on the floor, guarding the ball that was bigger and blacker than he was. He'd growl at the kid in the window.

Siebren turned to look at the imaginary kid, and the dream crashed. The woman had pulled the drapes apart, and she was looking at him. Her whole face was grinning. She'd seen him playacting and foolish.

It was too much change—too suddenly. He started crying. Pitifully he blurted out: "I . . . I couldn't button up. I've got a hurt thumb and I can't button with one hand."

He stopped and held the bloodied bandage up for her to see. Then, of their own accord, the words came rushing out: "How much is that big black ball?"

The two men went on talking. But the nice woman didn't laugh. She said softly, "Well now, one thing at a time. Everybody comes unbuttoned at times—let's see about that first."

He stepped mutely through the drapes she held back for him. Then she turned him around, stooped over his shoulder, and buttoned him—just the way his mother used to do when he was small. A welling of relief came so hard he had to lean the back of his thankful head against her for a touch of a moment.

She noticed. She kissed him on the top of his head, right in his hair—the way Mother did when she loved Knillis extra.

He loved her!

For the moment there was nothing to say, and they listened to the men. "Well now," the woman said. "You can see that those two are too busy for anything but church talk, so let's the two of us have a little tea party. But first let me look at that thumb. No use having a tea party and you bleeding to death and fading away right before my eyes." She clucked and jiggled and shook all her big body to show him it was a joke. Then she took the bandage off. Heads together, they studied the cut. She pinched it a little. "See," she said, "when you struggle with buttons and things, you squeeze it open, and it starts bleeding again. But it's a nice clean cut, and right after tea I'll bandage it—we'll let it air out a little. But first—what's your name? I always ask people their names before I bandage them up." She shook all over again. He loved her.

"My name's Siebren," he told her softly.

"Mine's Aal."

"Aal?" he asked carefully because knowing her name might make it easier to tell her about the cookies. "Aal," he said, "I took some cookies. But I didn't take them for me. It was for a little dog that Grandpa hit by mistake with his cane." He told her about bandaging Wayfarer's leg. "But that wasn't from

Grandpa hitting him." He looked at the cookies. Now that he wasn't scared and ashamed anymore, he was hungry! He told Aal about feeding his sandwiches to the little dog—all of them, every bite but one. Aal, listening, just handed him a cookie. He closed his mouth over the whole cookie, remembering just in time not to tell Aal about Wayfarer being in the schoolhouse. If Aal should tell Grandpa! Maybe, like Grandpa, Aal didn't like dogs either—only goldfish. You could be wonderful, he supposed, and still not like dogs.

Aal noticed that he'd stopped talking. She reached over, took the saucer from under his cup of tea, and filled it with a whole handful of cookies—an even bigger handful than he'd stolen. He munched another thick crisp cookie, then he had to talk about the big ball. He told Aal how badly he wanted the ball. He was honest and also told her that all he had was the seventeen cents from Grandpa—oh, and whatever there might be in his piggy bank at home.

Aal listened, and sipping her tea, she nodded somberly. "Yes, Siebren, I know how it is about wanting things. That's the way it is all your life. When I was a little girl your age, I wanted to be queen of the Netherlands, or at least a fat little princess. But I didn't get to be queen, not even a princess—just fat." Aal jiggled all over as they both giggled together about the funniness. Aal poured more tea with even more milk this time and two whole scoops of sugar, but she was shaking so, the sugar spilled. "Got to get a little something into you—all the way to that monastery in the night, and all your sandwiches inside a strange dog."

When Aal was that nice—two scoops of sugar and everything—Siebren dared to ask right out, "Aal, I don't know how much I've got in my bank at home, but there must be almost a gulden. Would that be enough? How much is the ball?"

"A queen's ransom, at least," Aal said straight-faced, "with two fat little princesses thrown in."

It was funny. It was funny even in the midst of it being most likely he could never have the big black ball. Oh, Aal was funny. He almost did not want to go to the monastery of that inland aunt if he could stay with Aal. And then Wayfarer would be right next door.

Aal half got up out of her chair as she said, "I can't think what's in your grandfather's mind. It'll be midnight before you get to the monastery, and finding your way in that watery mess. . . . But when those two get talking church talk, you could build a church and a steeple before they get through with their talk. Now I don't want you to get scared. I'm going to make a big fuss about that thumb of yours, but it's just to get those two out of their chairs."

Amazingly, Aal dug down through a slit in her skirt

into her pocket and fished out a whole shiny silver gulden. "Now this is between you and me," she explained. "Of course you can tell your grandpa after you get on the road. But as you can see we've just started this store, and my husband's no storekeeper—all he knows about is holes in the dike. He let some smart salesman talk him into buying that whole showcase of rubber balls—it's enough to keep Lahsens in rubber balls until the year two thousand. So the big black one is going to be his first sale, because it'll do him a whole mess of good. He has felt pretty foolish letting that smooth salesman talk him into all those balls. So, Siebren, you're going to buy that ball, and it'll be our very first sale."

He couldn't believe it. But Aal just reached over and pushed the big silver gulden into his pocket. The gulden slid down on top of the seventeen cents. It clanked. You could hear it. "Remember," Aal told him, "that's exactly what the ball's going to cost—my gulden and your seventeen cents. It's to bring us luck with the new store."

"Luck," Siebren said in a faraway voice, as if out of a dream. "Oh, luck! I know—" He grabbed in his back pocket with his good hand and whipped out the flattened chocolate tin. "Aal, this is how I got my sore thumb, and it's brought all kinds of good luck. It's for you—for luck." He thrust it at her eagerly, glad to see that most of the blood spots had worn off in his pocket.

"Child!" Aal said in a funny voice. She took it! She shoved it through the slit in her skirt, and it rattled into her deep pocket. "Child," she said again, and she didn't laugh. She bustled away fast. She came back in a moment with a pan of hot water, towels, and a roll of narrow bandage. She cleaned the cut. They didn't talk, but their heads were close together over the thumb. Even though it hurt, Siebren stood very quiet for Aal. She made him want to be good— oh, impossibly, perfectly good—inside and out.

"Now I'm going to call the two men," Aal warned, "and I'm going to show them the thumb and make a big fuss. But you leave it all to me; don't you say a thing." Then she called out through the drapes, "Listen, you two. There you sit hearing and seeing nothing—this child could have bled to death!"

There was an abrupt silence, then chairs scraped and both men came hurrying. Aal was ready for them. She showed them the old bandage that was now soggy and bloody wet because Aal had dribbled warm water on it. "Look," Aal scolded her husband, "there you sit and talk and talk, world without end. Didn't even know enough to give the child a cookie—just let him bleed."

The dike inspector bent his bald head over Siebren's thumb. "I didn't know," he mumbled. He swallowed, dropped Siebren's hand, and grabbed one of the cookies. "Here, have a cookie," he told Siebren. "Take it quick. Never could stand the sight of blood."

"Good evening, Aal," Grandfather said politely. He sounded like a little boy.

Aal humphed. She turned on her husband. "A cookie! Out of my way while I bandage this thumb. And if you can't stand to watch, you go get that big black ball out of the showcase. It's to cost one gulden and seventeen cents because that's how much Siebren has, and—well there's your first sale."

The bald-headed man was only too glad to go. Aal winked at Siebren, but he couldn't wink back—he could hardly breathe. The man was going for the ball.

Aal got busy with the bandage, and Grandfather stood over them, watching. Dithering inside, Siebren waited. He listened to every sound the inspector made at the showcase. Grandpa held his shoulders to keep him steady while Aal wound the bandage tight around his thumb. Siebren scarcely noticed. Then Aal took a needle and thread and sewed the neat bandage shut. "There," she said, "now you can even use your thumb a little, and it won't start to bleed every move you make."

He couldn't speak, he was waiting too hard. But to show Aal how grateful he was, he shoved his sore hand deep down in his pocket.

"Well, now," Aal said, "that's important. What kind of sissy is it walking without one or two hands in your pockets?"

He'd rammed his hand down on the gulden and

the seventeen cents, but it hadn't hurt. Aal's bandage was so slim and thin he could pull up the money between the bandaged thumb and two fingers. He had his money ready when the inspector shouldered the drapes aside. He *had* to use his shoulders because the ball was so big he had to hold it with both hands. He turned to Siebren. "If you please, little man," he said in his new storekeeper voice, "here is your ball."

Siebren put his own hands numbly around the ball, and the new bandage stood out whiter than white against its shiny blackness.

Grandfather said, "Well, Siebren, what do you say?"

Dumbly Siebren handed the man the gulden and the seventeen cents. He couldn't make a sound. His throat worked, but he couldn't even whisper. Grandfather looked hard at him.

Then nice Aal said to Grandpa, "Must the child still walk all the way to that monastery? He should have been in bed after the shock of that thumb. . . . Don't men ever think, except about dikes and churches?"

Grandfather laughed and put both hands up as if to ward Aal off. "All right, all right, we're on our way. The moon's going to be out later, so we'll have plenty of light by the time we get to the marsh."

With an arm around him, Aal pushed Siebren along as she talked. He held the big ball, and Grandfather and the dike inspector followed. Siebren was first outside. He stood and clutched the ball while everybody talked in the doorway.

When Grandpa stepped outside, he gave Siebren a nudge. "Can't you say anything?"

The nudge knocked the ball out of Siebren's hands. It helped somehow, for while running after the ball he found it easy to shout, "Oh thank you, thank you for everything and the ball."

"Stop on your way back," Aal called, and her husband nodded his bald head. Then Aal threw Siebren a kiss and firmly closed the door to stop all talk and get them on their way.

"Well," Grandpa said as he turned to go, "I'm glad that at last you could make yourself say thank you." He looked at the ball. "Now you've really got something to make you keep your thumb up—about the best thing in the world, I'd say, and worth a small, thin thank you."

Siebren nodded so hard his nose poked the ball. Oh, he'd never be able to talk, and he'd never deep inside believe the big ball was actually his. He was walking away from Wayfarer in the closed school, but he couldn't worry about that at this moment—not now, not now. He squeezed the ball and held it tight, and over its glossy rounding lay the whole dark night and the stillness of the whole sky without a star. And still everything shone—and everything sang.

7

The House at the Edge of the Marsh

"Now that was your last scare from those blasted farm dogs because that was the last farm." Finally Grandpa had stopped to wait for him.

"Won't there be a dog at the monastery?" Siebren asked in order to keep Grandpa standing still. He put the ball down between his feet. All the way out of Lahsens he'd had to jog trot through the gravel, but still he had always been way behind.

Oh, he was tired! He was asleep on his feet. It was good to stand still and let the scare from the last rushing farm dog seep out of him. He didn't know which was worse, their sudden ugly roar out of the blackness or the awful rattle of their long chains. The last big dog—the one that had made him call to Grandpa for help—had actually dragged his kennel by his chain to get at him.

He suddenly realized Grandpa had answered him. "What did you say, Grandpa?"

"Look, I've already answered you twice," Grandpa said impatiently. "I said that at the monastery you won't find a pup or a kit. Just frogs."

All he could do was stare, he was so tired. "Frogs? You walked so fast all the way," he complained, "I couldn't keep up—even running."

"That's because I was thinking," Grandpa said. "You'd think my mind was in my feet—the harder I think, the faster I walk. My friend Freerk told me of some ugly problems in the Lahsens church, and that struck sparks, and the harder I thought about it, the faster I walked, I guess."

"Even your cane struck sparks," Siebren told him. "I could follow you by the sparks you struck out of the flint stones in the gravel."

"Then from here on you'd better stay close. We're practically at the edge of the marsh, and then the road is just a couple of wagon tracks with humped dirt between—so no more sparks. If you see anything that looks like a spark, it'll be fireflies. The moon is all clouded over, so that's all the light you're going to see—fireflies. And all you'll hear is frogs—because that's all there is up ahead. Ten thousand thousand booming frogs and ten times that many fireflies—millions of fireflies."

"Ten thousand thousand frogs, a million fireflies," Siebren said in soft, slow delight.

"Well, I may have put it a little bit thick," Grandpa said and started off. "Now try to keep up," he ordered over his shoulder.

"Grandpa, I can't," Siebren said and stayed where he was. "It's because I've got to hold the ball with both hands, and then I can't swing my arms—just wriggle my shoulders. But if I wriggle too much, the ball squeezes out of my hands, and a black ball is hard to find in the dark. Then when I do find it, I've got to run again to catch up with you."

"Are you complaining?" Grandfather asked. "You wanted that ball, body and soul. But that often comes from worldly possessions; you long for them, but once you have them they're nothing but care and trouble." Grandpa got a queer look on his face. "Toss it away," he said offhandedly.

"NO!" Siebren screamed, so loud that the dog from the last farm they passed heard and began a wild barking.

"Can't you take a joke?" Grandpa said shortly.

He couldn't say that some things—like his proud ball—couldn't be made into a joke. But Grandpa was already gone up the road, and the road was a tunnel of gray under a sky that hung low over him. The dark leaned in all around.

Siebren stooped to pick up the ball, but his foot slipped, and he nudged the ball. It spurted away, making small snaky sounds over the gravel. He scuttled after it. When he found it on the dark roadside, he told the ball, "I hate you."

He stood aghast at his words. But he'd thought them long before he had said them. The ball made trouble. It kept squeezing out of his stiff tired hands; he'd have to find it, and then he had to run again to catch up.

Those fierce ugly farm dogs had let Grandpa pass, but when they heard him running, the black still night split with their roaring. It scared you so, even if they were chained, that it was as if your head split open and you saw light, and the whole night roared.

With the ball once more in his arms he jogged ahead to catch up with Grandpa, but he couldn't hear or see him. The cane wasn't striking sparks. "Grandpa—Grandpa!" he yelled. "Wait, Grandpa . . . wait . . . I . . . ."

He ran wildly ahead. Stones rolled and skittered under his feet, and he was flung headlong into the gravel. He lay there a second, bloody-nosed, then he pushed himself up from the cutting gravel. Grandpa came running. Siebren could see the ball rushing toward Grandpa, but he didn't have time to warn him. The ball hit. Grandpa jumped high, so high that the ball rolled under him and off to the side of the road.

"Blasted kid!" Grandpa yelled, startled, scared, and angry. "Do you have to play with that ball all the time? I thought it was something out of the swamp rushing at me."

"I fell. I've got a bloody nose," Siebren whimpered. But Grandpa did not come; he hurried after the ball. He was so angry maybe he'd kick it into the swamp. Siebren scrambled up and beat Grandpa to the ball. He scooped it up from under Grandpa's reaching hands.

"That ball!" Grandpa said. "Whatever made Aal give it to you?" Then he shook Siebren. "Your mother wasn't foolish enough to give you all that? Where did you get a whole gulden?"

Siebren had to hold his thumb with its bandage under his nose so he could answer without the blood running into his mouth. "Aal gave it to me," he said. Indignantly he whipped out the whole story—but Aal had said he could tell Grandpa once they were on the road. When he finished, Grandpa was silent.

"Ha," he said at last. "Ha, so that's how it went. My poor old friend Freerk, who, it seems to me, is going to be the most cheated storekeeper in the whole province, is cheated by you two on his very first sale.

Made a fool of! Made a fool of by my grandson and his own wife—you buying a ball from him with money out of his own pocket."

"No," Siebren explained, "it came out of Aal's pocket, the big one she keeps under her skirt."

"As if what comes out of Aal's pocket isn't the inspector's own."

"It was for good luck," Siebren pleaded. "It was the first sale; it was for good luck for the store Aal said."

"Luck," Grandpa snorted. "Well, I can't do anything about Aal—she's old enough to know better. But on the way back we'll return the ball, and you'll apologize to Freerk."

"But I didn't do it—it was Aal." That was treason. He loved Aal—but he'd said that! "Aal wanted me to have the ball," he finished lamely.

"So do I want you to have it, but I want you to own it honestly. If after you apologize to him, Freerk still wants you to have it too, then you can start saving for it with the seventeen cents I gave you. After you've saved enough, we'll come back together and fetch the ball. I promise you."

"How old will I be then?" Siebren asked in rebellion.

"Old enough to know better than to cheat," Grandpa said. "Now let's get on—but no more playing with that ball."

108

Siebren sniffed. Grandfather tried to peer at him through the dark to see if he was crying. He wouldn't cry! He was too angry to cry; he was sniffing because of his bloody nose. He'd be hanged if he'd tell Grandpa again that his nose was bleeding—he'd told him once. Grandpa'd see—if he bled to death. And he wouldn't keep up with Grandpa. It was better way back in the dark. The dark was scary, but it wasn't unfair and mean. Grandpa was. Grandpa wouldn't even listen. All right, he'd lose the ball in the swamp—that's what he'd do. He wasn't going to give it back and shame Aal. He'd tell his little inland aunt about Grandpa. Maybe she was nice like Aal. No, she was Grandpa's sister.

Siebren trudged tiredly along, hurrying only when an occasional spark struck by Grandfather's cane seemed too far ahead. He dragged—it was the only way he knew to defy Grandpa. He hugged the ball. It was funny in a way—a while ago he'd hated the ball, but now it was his proud possession again. It was good to feel proud. If he'd only kept the little chocolate tin, he'd feel even better. Everything had gone wrong since he'd given it away. It was a mean thought. He'd given it to Aal and he loved Aal—but he felt mean now.

It wasn't fair. Grandpa wasn't fair. He stumbled along in the dark, wanting to keep as far from Grandpa as possible. He pushed out his tongue, but not quite in Grandpa's direction. Anyway, he just didn't care!

At that moment Grandpa's cane struck a spark—Grandpa was far ahead. He didn't care; he wouldn't hurry. He stood still. Just how did you apologize? He didn't know how—and anyhow it wasn't his fault. Could he ask his aunt how to apologize to Freerk, even if she was Grandpa's sister? He stared ahead.

There now—look there! Wasn't that a house? Sure it was, so Grandfather had cheated too. He had even lied—out-and-out lied. He'd said there were no more farmhouses. Well, here was one, and Grandpa had walked right past it, but he hadn't called out, "Oh, Siebren, I told you wrong, here is the last farmhouse." If that wasn't cheating!

He couldn't resist it. There wasn't any sound of a dog, so he walked as far as the gate, set his feet wide, and yelled as loud as he could. "Hey, Grandpa! You said no more farms, but here is one!" He couldn't keep the crowing out of his voice.

In the dark house there was a crash. A door burst open so hard it hit the wall, and then there was light from inside. In the light a dog, big as a lion, came through the doorway in one lunging leap. The dog smashed the gate open. Siebren tried to ward off the huge animal with the ball, but the ball was smashed out of his hands and he was hurled backward down in the gravel.

110

For seconds his mind didn't work, then he knew he was under the great dog, but it—it was a puppy! It was uttering all kinds of glad, happy puppy cries it was so happy to see him. It was making a great game of worrying Siebren's hands off his face so it could lick him. Lick, lick, and lick. It whimpered puppy greetings, but it was so big and strong it held Siebren down. Its whip-waving tail swung so hard it rocked Siebren.

He opened his mouth to yell, but the puppy's wet tongue slap-slobbered into his mouth. It was so awful and yet at the same time so foolish that Siebren managed to push the big head away and say, "Get off me, you big fool. You get off me!"

The puppy went wild with delight at the sound of Siebren's voice. He wriggled so hard he squeezed all the breath out of Siebren's body, and there was nothing Siebren could do.

A cry came from the house. It was a woman's voice. "Who's there at the gate? Answer me—answer or I'll shoot."

At the woman's voice the big dog lashed his tail and wriggled even more joyously, but it made no move to get off Siebren. Siebren had no breath in his flattened, squeezed body to call out a word.

"Then I shoot," the woman screamed. "Then take this!"

With all his strength, Siebren twisted his face away

from the dog and saw a woman in the lighted doorway, holding a shotgun. She had an apron on over her nightgown, and she was taking shells from her pocket and slamming them into the gun. She put the gun to her shoulder and shot into the night. The flash of the gun split the darkness as she shot off both barrels. The recoil sent her staggering across the stoop, but already she was grabbling for more shells.

Siebren couldn't call out because now the great dog was on him, trying to bury itself. He lay flat over Siebren and worked his head into Siebren's neck, muffling Siebren's mouth and nose so Siebren could make no sound. In a piteous puppy voice the dog begged for the dreadful gun sounds to stop. Siebren clapped both hands over the dog's ears. Gratefully the dog lay still; only his long bony legs quivered.

Now Grandfather came running, shouting as he ran: "Griet, Griet! Stop! Stop that shooting! You're shooting at my grandson."

"Who's that?" The woman's voice quavered.

"Griet, calm yourself. It's David—David Rentema. You know me—we used to be neighbors. Where's Siebren? SIEBREN!"

Siebren managed to push the dog's head away enough to answer. "I'm all right, Grandpa. I'm here —under a dog—but he's scared of the shooting."

"I would think so," Grandpa called, relieved. "I'm scared out of seven years' growth myself. I thought

112

you were right behind me, and then the whole sky lit up with Griet's cannonading."

Grandpa came running. The woman came too, but she still carried the gun. She came on bare feet over the gravel and tried to pull the dog off Siebren. But at sight of the gun the poor thing was so shaken that she and Grandpa together couldn't pull him off. He made woeful noises. "I don't mind," Siebren said. "Just let me pet the shakes out of him. He's so scared he even wet."

Griet tried to lift him with her arms around his great chest. Two shells tumbled out of her pocket. "Grab them quick," she screamed. "If Landsake gets his jaws on them, we'll all go up in a blaze of powder. He chews everything!"

Landsake thought it was a new game, and all his fear vanished. He was all over Siebren to get the shells out of his hand. But by then Grandpa had his belt off, had run it through Landsake's collar, and was buckling the dog to the gate.

"Good," Griet said. "If your belt doesn't fly into seventeen pieces. . . . Well, David, I take it you're going to see your monastery sister." She wiped her hair back from her forehead. "Landsakes what excitement!" She took the bottom of her apron and wiped Siebren's face. "I expect he washed you good," she said, "so I ought to wipe you good. How'd you like to have him? You'd never have to wash your face again

114

—he'd even wash behind your ears. . . . Do you know he broke the door to get at Siebren?" she told Grandpa. "He's a fool over children—and here I got him to protect an old woman like me. If children wanted to break my windows, I think he'd bring them the stones in his mouth. He's a big mooncalf, but I love him. He chews my furniture, but he's the best company in the world. Goodness, how I'm babbling! I'm that upset—me shooting at a child lying helpless at my gate."

"It's all right now, Griet. No harm done," Grandpa said slowly to calm her. "I didn't even warn Siebren about your house because it isn't a farmhouse with a guard dog—in fact the last I knew, you had a fuzzy mop of a lapdog—and just about as much good as a mop—to defend you."

"He died," Griet said. "And when my mother died, you see, I came out here to keep house for my father. But now he's dead too, and I'm all alone at the edge of this marsh. I figured I needed a terror of a dog, so I got a Great Dane. But look at him—he loves everybody. So then I got a shotgun, and so that everyone will know I have it, I shoot both barrels every night before I go to bed. Landsake just crawls under the bed when I shoot—it hurts his ears, I guess. Well, it hurts my shoulder. It's black-and-blue and hurts like sin, but I keep on shooting every night to scare everything off."

"Griet, don't do it anymore. Everyone knows about your bedtime shooting. I heard of it in Weirom, but I couldn't believe it. All you're doing is announcing your bedtime to the countryside. The dog is enough."

"Well, David, I suppose he *could* knock them down and lick them to death." She laughed.

"He wouldn't have to do anything," Grandpa told her. "Why, they just have to see him—or know about him. His size is enough, isn't it, Siebren?"

"*I* thought he was a lion," Siebren said.

"He's still only a puppy," Grandpa said, "but will grow into a power of a dog with a roar like a real lion. He's all you need, Griet."

"Do you think so—do you really think so?"

"I know so," Grandfather said.

"Oh, then—then take these with you—they're my last." Griet handed the shotgun shells to Grandpa. "I'll rub some liniment on my shoulder and go to sleep. You always were a comfort to me, David Rentema, when I was your neighbor in Weirom. But now with just the marsh for a neighbor, I'm scared. The awfullest cries and the scariest sounds come out of it in the night."

"I know, I know," Grandpa said. "But the cries sound dangerous just because the criers are so harmless and helpless. It's just sound effects to scare you away—the way you tried to scare everything with your shotgun."

116

"Is that so, David?" Griet said wonderingly. "Ah, if you say so, it is so. You were always to be believed. I'll sleep well tonight—for the first time in weeks."

She unbuckled Landsake from the gate and handed Grandpa his belt. "The swamp's bad enough in the dark without having to hold up your pants with both hands," she said mildly. "Well, if you'll excuse me, I'm going in the house and sleep and sleep. Say good-bye to Siebren, Landsake."

"Run," Grandpa said. "I'll latch your gate."

Siebren put his hand on the huge dog's head. "Good-bye, Landsake," he said. "She isn't going to shoot anymore—ever. Oh, but you're a good dog!"

The puppy wriggled with joy. Then Griet led him away by his heavy collar, and the dog's thick tail lashed her joyously all the way as they hurried to their sleep.

Grandfather locked the gate.

8

The Little Woman
in the Marsh

Siebren was proud of his grandfather. Grandpa hadn't
cheated, hadn't lied—he just hadn't known Griet had
such a dog as Landsake. And Griet had known that
Grandpa's word was sure and true. She'd said right
out, "If you say so, David, then it's so."

It made you so proud the feeling sat big in your
chest. And after Grandfather had closed the gate and
they'd started out, he had even retrieved the ball when
he—Siebren—had forgotten it in the excitement with
Landsake. Hey, it must mean Grandfather wanted
him to have the ball! Maybe it even meant he
wouldn't have to apologize to the dike inspector.

"Well," Grandfather said out of the dark up ahead, "I've always made this journey by night, and it's always been as calm and common as ditchwater, but with you along there seems to be something doing every minute."

Siebren laughed, but he didn't tell Grandpa that it was the luck of the chocolate tin. Grandpa didn't believe in luck; Grandpa believed in God. He would say that God wouldn't mess around with little for-free chocolate tins. But wasn't it funny how Grandpa changed and changed? Now he was a friend again and a comfort in the dark. It was all because Grandfather hadn't cheated or lied—that would have been awful.

"Oh, I wish we were at the monastery," he called out.

"The only way we'll get there is by stepping ahead one foot at a time, then pulling the back foot along," Grandpa joked.

Siebren was too busy thinking to laugh. Funny— you wanted the biggest ball, but not the biggest dog. He wanted only Wayfarer—he'd ask the little aunt how to keep Wayfarer.

"Grandpa," he called out chummily, "did you hear what Griet said? She asked did I want Landsake. I've got the biggest ball, and he's the biggest dog—but I like little dogs better."

"Well, Griet was only fooling; she loves that dog. But let's not moon around about dogs and balls now because right here where I'm standing we turn into the wagon path that's going to lead us through the marsh."

"There's the first firefly," Siebren announced.

"The first of ten hundred thousand, but that's where the marsh really begins—at the first firefly. Watch them though when we get into the swamp. They're always at the water's edge, so we'll have them on both sides of the wagon path. But don't follow them! They're miserable little cheats and will lead you down into the water. Stay in the middle of the wagon path. No more mooning about balls and dogs." Grandpa started down the humped narrow path between the two wagon ruts.

"There aren't hardly any fireflies," Siebren called out just to hear Grandpa's voice. It was quiet on the dirt path. There wasn't any crunch of gravel—only black stillness.

"There isn't any water yet either," Grandpa answered. "The wagon path is just beginning to lead us into the marsh. But even then it's just a very shallow marsh, and all a marsh really is is reeds and brush and water lilies and eelgrass and pickerelweed —with water standing among everything. The water won't be deep, and the marsh can even look like a grassy meadow, but water is everywhere. And the really dangerous thing is that under the water is the muck, and to the muck there is no end. It's bottomless. If you land in it, the more you struggle, the more you go down, until even a stork flying high overhead couldn't find you again."

"Grandpa, you sound awful," Siebren said in a hollow voice. "Grandpa, why do you talk so awful here? You told Mother there was nothing to going through the marsh if you knew the path."

"That's exactly it," Grandpa said. "That's what I want to impress on you. Stay on the path. Stay right behind me, and if you make a misstep and your foot touches soft, yielding grass, pull that foot back as fast as you can. And watch the fireflies—where they're the thickest that's land's edge—fireflies don't seem to go much out over the water. They mark the shore."

Siebren wondered bleakly if Grandpa would let him hang onto the end of the cane. It was too babyish to ask Grandpa to carry him. "Grandpa, I want to go home." The words had pressed out in spite of him. And he didn't care if it sounded like crying. He wasn't crying, but he felt like crying.

Grandpa laid his big hand on Siebren's shoulder. "Don't be scared," he said gently. "I may have put it on a bit thick, but the swamp is that way, and I talked that way so you wouldn't be careless one moment—you're such a mooner. But I know the swamp and love it, and your little aunt loves it—and she wouldn't love it if it were only awful, now would she? Tomorrow by daylight you'll see how beautiful it can be. Stay right behind me, and if you should drop the ball, let it roll. Your aunt knows the marsh like I know the back of my hand, and in her little skiff that's hardly bigger than a toy she'll take you through the marsh and find the ball for you."

"If the boat's that little, will it hold me too?"

"It'll hold you. It skims over water and over grass, and your aunt knows every unseen channel, every wild duck's nest, and where the herons stand and the white storks hunt for frogs. You'll see it all tomorrow."

"Are we staying all day tomorrow?"

"At least tomorrow, and maybe part of the next day."

"I want to go," Siebren decided. He couldn't help it that he sounded like a little changing child. First Grandpa scared him, and then he made it sound almost too wonderful.

"Of course you want to go," Grandpa told him. "Now then, see the dark that looms like a wall ahead of us? Well, it's not a wall. It's thick trees on a ridge around the rim of the swamp. Behind the trees the marsh begins. Once we come over the ridge and down through the trees, the whole life of the swamp will burst in on you. So many frogs will boom so hard it's like a crashing roar. And above the frogs you'll hear the faraway cries of night birds and little swamp animals. Don't worry, the cries will stay far beyond us because as we come blundering, everything around us will go still. Everything is scared of us. Except the fireflies—there'll still be ten hundred thousand fireflies, and they'll be all around our heads as if to light our way."

"Oh, Grandpa," Siebren said. "Grandpa, I'm glad I came. It's the most wonderful trip!" He was amazed that his stern, strict grandfather could have wonderful words to make such wonderful pictures.

Grandpa patted Siebren's shoulder. "Fine, then over the ridge and into the marsh we go. And even if you get as old as I am now, you'll never forget coming over the ridge and down into the marsh. That's how I came more than sixty years ago—to live two years with my little sister. That was before I was married myself. . . . I wanted you, my first grandson, to come to the marsh in the night, the way I came. The moon should have been out, but you can't have everything, and even so you'll never forget."

Then Grandpa stepped out toward the ridge of the black trees. But he turned. "Hey, those bandages! I just now thought of them. We'll make a rope of them with me on one end and you on the other. I'd let you hang onto my cane, but I need it to feel my way—and the bandage-rope will be better."

Swiftly Grandfather knotted the bandages he'd dug out of his pocket. Then Siebren, clutching the ball in one arm, hung onto the bandage-rope with his good hand, and at the end of his white rope trudged on behind Grandpa.

"Thank you, Grandpa," he mumbled. "Thank you,

thank you." He clutched the big ball. Oh, grandpas were all kinds of things, stern and strict and teasing, sometimes even fun, then sometimes wonderful.

Now he would go exactly where Grandpa went, at his end of the bandage-rope. He gave the ball a soft quick kiss so Grandfather wouldn't hear him being silly. Oh, tomorrow he'd tell everything to his little aunt, sitting in the boat with her, going through the marsh, because the marsh would be a whole new world. In that new world you'd be doing such new things that surely you could say and tell things you could never tell on Peppermint Street.

They were through the trees. The water of the marsh lay before them, a great flat sheet of endlessness, and that endlessness boomed out in one great roar.

Those were the frogs. Then there were the fireflies, thousands of fireflies. They darted and flitted as if lifted on the great roaring boom of the frogs.

Grandpa let Siebren stand and look. "Now you see it the way I saw it the first time I came. I came by night too, and I didn't know the marsh, but I found my way. So follow me. I'll be the old lead horse at the end of the rope, and you the prancing colt."

Siebren had no words. There were no words. It was scary, but somehow that made it even more wonderful.

124

They were in the marsh. Now the wagon path had water on either side of it, and the fireflies flitted close. But where he and Grandpa walked, the marsh went silent. The frogs abruptly stopped booming and made little splashes as they dived for safety. But the fireflies went on crisscrossing the wagon path. One landed for a brief glowing moment on the ball, and before it closed its wings, the black ball gleamed its reflection. The firefly rested on the ball. There was no sound anywhere nearby; then there was the sudden squish-squash of Grandpa's wooden shoes in water.

"The road's sunken here," Grandpa warned. "There's water, but it doesn't go over your shoes. This marsh road does that—sort of caves in and goes under but never very far." Grandpa poked and sounded with his cane, then edged ahead. "Watch where you step; if it goes over your shoes, yell out, and we'll poke around and find a sounder edge of the path."

On the ball the firefly opened its wings. Its gleam came on and glowed in the glossiness of the ball. Siebren watched in delight. Then Grandpa did what he had told *him* not to do. Grandfather went down into deep muck. He hadn't pulled back as he'd said to do! He'd taken that next step. Now there was no path where Grandpa was—only a black welling of water.

Grandfather plunged in greater steps. His steps made sucking noises, and Grandpa made great hoarse gasping sounds as the cold water came up. He plunged wilder and wilder. In between his awful steps and the frightening sounds of his breathing, he kept gasping out orders: "Siebren—back, back. Let go of the rope. Don't come . . . Siebren, back . . . back."

"Grandpa, stop taking steps," Siebren screamed. "You said don't take steps. Grandpa, don't! Grandpa!"

He stood bawling while Grandpa plunged like a wild mired steer and made awful moolike sounds with his hard breathing. Now he could hardly pull one leg up as the other went down, but he still kept struggling toward a round spot straight ahead that looked like thick grass. Then he reached the little island of grass and lay over it, his legs all sunken away. He put his cane across the grass and pressed down on it to hold himself up, but the tiny island wasn't solid. It was grass on water, and it sank under the cane. Grandpa's face went into the floating grass.

"The ball!" Siebren screamed. "Won't the ball hold you up? Here comes the ball!" With water running over his shoes, he sent the ball swishing toward Grandpa. Grandpa pushed himself up long enough to sweep the ball in with one arm. Then he put both hands on the big ball and pressed down; it didn't go under, and Grandpa didn't go down any more. His face was up from the water, and he was still. Oh, but he was still, except for his hard breathing. But he wasn't making the awful moolike sounds anymore.

"It's holding," Siebren bawled out. "It's holding."

"It's holding," Grandpa answered between swallows of air. "That was quick thinking. I guess it was the only thing that could have kept me from going down."

Then Grandpa was silent so he could rest, and they were both so still that the frogs came back.

At last Grandpa made a joke. "And here I took a bath before we came—why couldn't I have waited for this?"

Grandpa could joke in such a place! Siebren laughed a little for Grandpa's sake. Then he couldn't stop. He shrieked with laughter.

Grandpa twisted, and with only one hand on the ball, scooped up water and splashed it over Siebren in one shocking spray. "Now don't go to pieces when it's all over."

The slosh of cold water stopped the laugh, and Siebren asked, cold sober, "But what are we going to do now?"

Pushing down on the ball, Grandpa looked around. "I could maybe make it back to you buoyed up by the ball, but this old heart and these stiff legs have had enough. Suppose you yell for help. Your high voice will carry, and maybe your aunt will hear you. The monastery's not too far away, and then she will come with the boat."

"What do I do, just call 'HELP'?" Siebren asked.

"No, that might sound too awful coming up out of the swamp in the dead of night. Call your aunt's name."

Siebren didn't wait; he screamed out Aunt Hinka's name so sharp, so high, the whole marsh fell silent in all its far reaches. Siebren's voice screeched over the water: "AUNT HINKA, AUNT HINKA."

Surprisingly, at once there came a hallooing answer. Close! "Coming. I'm coming. Keep calling, keep calling."

"Where is she?" Siebren asked, amazed.

"She must have been out in her boat," Grandpa said. "She does that sometimes. Hinka," Grandfather bawled. "It's David, your brother, stuck in the muck."

She had come silently, and from right nearby she answered, "Why, you old fool. That isn't going to do much for your rheumatism." There was the small sound of oars. "It's a good thing I started out when I heard Griet's shooting. She'd already shot her bedtime shots, so when she shot again, I got in the boat to see if I could help. But who'd think you'd be cowblundering around in the marsh?"

"If you'd only keep your road up out of the water," Grandpa joked.

In a soft swift glide Aunt Hinka was there. She picked up a lantern out of the bottom of the boat, held it high, saw Grandpa, and putting the lantern down, turned the narrow little skiff and sent it backward straight at Grandpa. Grandpa caught the boat as it bore down upon him. Its speed helped him pull his leg out of the sucking muck. He threw himself, chest flat over the end of the boat, grabbed hold of the edge of a seat, and pulled himself into the skiff. Aunt Hinka steadied the rocking boat with a push pole she set against the grass hummock where Grandpa had gone down.

"But I thought I heard a child," she said.

"That was me," Siebren called. "Aunt Hinka, I'm here. I'm Siebren."

"Well, Siebren!" she said. "What a way to meet. And you took Siebren in here in the dead of the night?" she said to Grandpa.

"I thought I knew the road," Grandpa said.

"Nobody knows the road," she said. "You may not have had them along the sea, but we've had heavy rains here, and when the marsh rises with rain, the road goes under."

"Can we all get in the boat?" Grandpa asked. "If not, take Siebren first."

"Not on your life," the little woman said. "You and your heart down in that water! And I see you even need a cane for your rheumatism now—saw one floating. No, you first. We'll just be gone minutes, and there's no harm in the swamp. Just frogs and fireflies and some birds. . . . All right, Siebren?" she asked. "You won't be scared? I'll be right back."

"Grandpa, may I have the ball?" Siebren asked in a small voice.

"The ball?" Grandpa said. "Oh sure, the ball." He twisted around in the boat, saw the floating ball, and made as if to reach for it. Aunt Hinka pushed him back in his seat. "Unless you want to go cow-walking in the muck again, you sit still," she told Grandpa severely. "This is not a steamer." Then she neatly flipped the ball with her oar. It swished across the water so straight and true Siebren didn't have to move. It came rushing up the sunken path to him.

"There's your ball," Grandpa said. "And Siebren, you know, don't you, that it won't go back to the store? I want to pay for it myself. It saved my life."

Aunt Hinka must have fished the cane out of the water, for Grandpa suddenly sent it arrowing to the spot where Siebren stood. "Have the cane too. I know it'll make you feel safer—although there's nothing to harm you here in the marsh, as your aunt told you."

"About the only thing would be if a frog should jump too high and land down your throat," Aunt Hinka said cheerfully. "And don't mind the night noises, strange and wicked as they sound. They're only from night birds making brave sounds because they're so scared. . . . But that's an idea, Siebren. If the marsh

130

sounds scare you, make up your own noises and scare everything in the swamp. You just sing. Sing, and I'll be back in just a few songs."

"Sing?" Siebren asked. "What can I sing? I can't sing in a marsh."

For answer his little aunt began singing. It was a song Siebren had never heard before. It had the craziest words:

> There once were seven little frogs,
> All in a dried-up ditch;
> There came a man in wooden shoes,
> But elsewhere not a stitch.

Siebren giggled, but the boat was going away. To hold it a little longer he called, "What's the rest of it?"

"Oh," Aunt Hinka said, "the rest's so awful I wouldn't dare sing it—not in the middle of the night, in the middle of a marsh." Then she sang the little song over again, and Grandpa joined in with his hoarse old voice. But Aunt Hinka stopped the song in the middle. "Siebren, you're not singing with us. Sing, don't doubt! We always wait because we doubt, because we don't believe. So do it now—sing with us, then you'll believe that singing helps when you're alone."

"I won't be scared," he said hoarsely.

"Yes you will, once you're alone. It isn't small and

131

silly to be scared, Siebren. I'm not talking to you like a big grown-up person and just telling you something. I believe this myself. I know it works to sing when you're afraid. I know because I'm a small person and often scared. I stayed small, so then I had to learn tricks that people who grow big never need."

He stood with his mouth open, listening. He stood, mouth open, believing. He believed her because she didn't talk like a grown-up and tell him just anything to get rid of him. She was even smaller than he, but she was old—so she knew. She was old and knew what it was to be scared, yet she didn't flip away scaredness as if it were nothing.

Because of her he wanted to sing. He sang with them, and singing with him they went away, but now it didn't seem so alone. Each time the song was finished they started right over again, and all the time the boat was getting farther away. A little later Siebren realized he was singing alone—they were gone.

His song faltered. He couldn't sing now, but it helped to think about his little aunt. She was so tiny and thin, yet she had come through the black marsh all alone when she'd heard Griet's shotgun—all alone and so little. And she was old—ah, but that was it! That was the difference! She was old and knew, so she wasn't afraid.

"Old and knew," Siebren said wonderingly. Hey, they fit together, like old and new. He made it into a hasty sort of song, and under his breath he sang the one line over and over. Then he actually settled himself on the hump in the middle of the wagon path between the deep wheel ruts. He hugged his knees to his chest. He squeezed the cane between his knees. The ball lay tight against him; the lantern stood—warm with its light—close to his other side. It wasn't good, though, to be quiet; he sang his one-line song again. If he didn't sing, he could hear the watery muck, where Grandpa had gone down, still making dark ugly noises. There were filthy plopping sounds when great welling black bubbles broke—it was just as if a giant were breathing under the muck. A giant . . . Siebren thought of the big deaf-and-dumb uncle. He hastily started to sing again.

An owl, or something fierce and horrible, cried far across the swamp. Horror rose higher and higher in its screeching call, then the calls went low and weepy and spooky. Siebren's song stopped in his mouth. The owl, or whatever awfulness, also stopped. Now everything was unnaturally still, and clouds swept low. He sat very small.

The horrible owl started up again. Suddenly Siebren sang out fiercely at the owl—for his little aunt's sake, for his brave little aunt. He made his one-line song go up and down the way the owl screeched high and low:

Old *and*   *old* *and*
     knew—   *new.*

It made it fun; it made it brave. It was a little nothing song, but it was brave. When his throat felt tired from singing the one-line song up and down, he began to sing the naked-frog song over and over. He kept count. And it was when he had sung the silly song thirty-eight times that suddenly—near—his aunt began singing along. Siebren jumped up. His aunt poled the light little boat right up the slope of the wagon path where he and the lantern stood.

"Well now, didn't that song help?" Aunt Hinka asked. "It's a silly song for courage. My mother taught it to me when I was a child—it's such an old nonsense song."

Siebren hurriedly put the ball, the cane, and the lantern in the boat and crawled onto the back seat. "But it has no end," he breathed.

"I guess nonsense has no end—but there really isn't any more to the song."

"But I know an end," he told her. "I made an end while I was singing, because when I puzzled over it, then I wasn't so scared. Shall I tell you what happened?"

"If you want me to breathe, you should tell me. I sang the song all my life and never knew an end— you can't leave me that high in the air."

"Oh," he said, delighted. "Oh, it's only that the naked man with the wooden shoes stayed to live in the ditch with the seven frogs because the frogs were naked too—and they didn't even have wooden shoes. So the man whittled seven little pairs of wooden shoes for the seven frogs. Then they weren't so naked anymore, and they lived happily together in the ditch and never got wet feet—even when there were heavy rains."

His little aunt threw up both her hands, and her laugh pealed out and tinkled away over the flat of the water. She had the loveliest laugh! "But that's a wonderful ending for an awful song. However did you think it up? And talking about frogs—did you know that you and your grandpa will sleep in a big bed in the living room? It's a room with a well. And in the well is a frog, so if you can't go right to sleep, you can sing the naked-frog song, and the real frog in the well will boom along to keep you company. It'll be almost like having a drum."

"But why do you have a well in the living room—and a frog in the well?"

"Well, the cistern is there, I guess, because the monks dug it there for their monastery a thousand or so years ago. But I put the frog in the cistern. I keep him for company; it's such a big stony lonesome house. But then Vrosk—that's his name—booms up out of his cistern and fills the whole house with sound."

"Oh, I want to see him. I can, can't I—still see him tonight?"

"Well then, take this pole and push us free, and

off we go. . . . Siebren, I can see you and I are going to have fun—songs and fun."

He pushed the boat free and sat down on the narrow seat. He all but wriggled like Landsake—he was so happy with her.

9

The Frog, Vrosk

There was a flat cold slap on the water, and drops splashed in Siebren's face. As he shuddered awake he heard a thin squealy scream as if from some child. "I . . . I fell asleep," Siebren said. "It's scary here. I heard a baby."

"No, that was a frog," Aunt Hinka said grimly. "I accidentally took the boat through a reedbed and scared a frog out of the reeds. A big pike must have been lurking, and as the frog jumped, the pike caught him in the air."

"A baby cried," Siebren insisted in sleepy stubbornness.

"No," Aunt Hinka said, "it was the last cry of the frog."

Siebren sat up straight and stared at the water still rippling in circles where the pike had gone down. "Oh, he must have been big," he said slowly. "He splashed water in my face way up here in the boat."

"No, I did, trying to brain the pike with my oar," Aunt Hinka told him. "I hate pike. Eating frogs is one thing, but these big marsh pike eat little ducklings right off the surface of the water. I've seen a little stream of wild ducklings swimming on behind their mother in a single yellow row, then suddenly one gets pulled down by his paddling feet, never to come up again. That's pike! I've seen a bird sit on a bending reed; a pike hurls himself into the air and brings the bird down. I hate pike! Tomorrow you and I will see if we can catch this monster, then we'll eat HIM—oh, slowly!"

"Alive?" Siebren yelled out in wide-awake alarm.

Aunt Hinka laughed. "No, fried slowly in butter and six beaten eggs . . . well, that woke you! But, Siebren, you mustn't fall asleep again in this shallow narrow boat. I was too busy to notice you were sleeping, but you could easily tumble out—so stay awake!"

Siebren, thinking of the monstrous pike, clutched the edges of the narrow boat, but the back end was riding so deep his fingers touched the water. What if a pike should come to the blood smell on his thumb and rip the whole thumb off? He cuddled his hands in his lap and hunched himself tightly, chills going up his spine.

"No, don't go hunching yourself for sleep," Aunt Hinka warned. "Maybe you'd better hold the big ball in your hands. If the ball rolls overboard, I'll know that you've gone to sleep again."

Siebren picked up the ball. He eyed the little boat mistrustfully. It was so little and short and narrow. The sides just fitted him and no more. Aunt Hinka, on the other seat, was so close their knees almost touched. But when she bent over the oars, the lantern light shining up from the bottom touched her small face and made it glow soft and sweet-safe.

Slowly the effortless slide of the boat became the glide of a dream through the night. There was no sound but the silvery spill-tinkle of waterdrops that fell from the lifted oars. The droplets made tiny tinkles before they smoothed themselves out to belong again to the flat sheet of marsh water.

Siebren heard himself yawning, six big cracking yawns in a row.

Aunt Hinka smiled. "Maybe we'd better sing. That should keep us awake."

Siebren poked around in his mind for the frog song, but he was so dull-worn for sleep he couldn't remember a word. He'd sung it thirty-eight times, and now it was gone. He'd sing Pieter Klimstra's cheap cap song for Aunt Hinka—that was funny too. He yawned again, and his mind stopped. "I can't think," he told her.

"Well, then I'll sing," she said. "You just try to sing along between yawns."

In a sweet, tinkly voice Aunt Hinka began to sing the counting-out song, the same song the kids in Weirom sang to see who was to be *It*. She knew it all.

> *Amsterdam, that great big town,*
> *Has been built on poles.*
> *Now if that big town should fall down,*
> *Who's to pay?*
> *You or me?*
> *No, you go free,*
> *And I pay for Amsterdam.*

The second time Aunt Hinka began, Siebren sang with her, surprised that old as she was his aunt knew the counting-out song. It must go back a long way. Thinking about Amsterdam built on poles, Siebren wondered if the monastery in the watery marsh was built on poles too. He pictured the little boat going under the monastery among great wooden posts like pillars. Way under there'd be a rope ladder. Clinging to the swaying, swinging ladder, he and his little aunt would climb through a trapdoor in the floor, and there they'd be, inside the great stone monastery.

He could hardly wait to finish the song to ask about the rope ladder up to the monastery. But after singing, Aunt Hinka started talking. "You know the song too? So it's still going on. That song must be as old as Amsterdam. I don't really know whether Amsterdam is built on poles, do you? I ought to know—as often as I've paid for it." Aunt Hinka laughed. "I was the littlest, and the big kids always made the song come out so I'd be *It* and pay for Amsterdam."

"You too?" Siebren crowed out. "Me too! I always have to be *It* for tag or hide-and-seek or anything. Oh, I'm not the littlest, but I always have to sit with Knillis, my baby brother, so when once in awhile I can play, I'm always *It*."

"Well," Aunt Hinka said. "It sounds like you and I own Amsterdam together."

"Yeah!" he said delightedly. It felt warm and chummy in the little boat with his little aunt, knowing she'd always been made to be *It* too. He wasn't going to ask if the monastery was on poles—he wasn't going to ask anything. He wanted to *tell* Aunt Hinka something in the great big chumminess. "And tomorrow we're going to fish for that big pike," he told her. "Let's go early—the very first thing—the two of us together."

"Child, it's early in the morning right now," Aunt Hinka said. "I made your grandfather soak his rheumatic old legs in a tub of hot water almost the minute he walked through the door, but the minute I get you through the door, you're both going to be marched straight to bed. You'll sleep until you can sleep no more—even if you sleep until noon. If that miserable pike can't wait until noon to be caught and eaten, that's his hard luck. And if Vrosk, the bullfrog in the cistern, utters a word in your room, I'll quiet him if I have to take him to bed with me."

Siebren looked at her with such astonishment that she threw back her head and laughed like a little girl. Of course he knew it was a joke, but he *was* going to sleep with Grandpa in a room with a bullfrog booming in a cistern. He sagged down on the seat in delight. He didn't want to ask anything. It was like a dream, with the dream gliding the way he was gliding over the water.

He hadn't seen a thing when suddenly Aunt Hinka said, "Here we are. Welcome to the monastery." She twisted the little boat about sharply, and Siebren faced the monastery. He sat staring and let his little aunt jump out and pull up the boat. The monastery rose up out of the flat marsh, somber and big and dark, but it was nothing but an enormous big farmhouse. "Welcome to my personal monastery," Aunt Hinka said.

He held the ball, not getting up, not picking up the lantern. It was an old farmhouse. He'd never been so disappointed in his life.

Aunt Hinka pulled him and the boat higher up the rise of land. She thought he was sleepy. "Are you waking up?" she asked.

Siebren nodded his head, picked up the lantern and the cane, and climbed out of the boat. They climbed toward the stone house at the top of the man-made hill. He felt stiff and slow. He'd seen old farmhouses before. The world was full of old farmhouses.

Of course they wouldn't be climbing up any swinging rope ladder through any trapdoor! Before them was nothing but a regular old farmhouse door. When Aunt Hinka opened it, it led into a kitchen. But Grandpa wasn't sitting there soaking his feet; Grandpa sat at the table with his hat on, ready to go. He stepped over and took the cane and the lantern. "I'll need them," he said to Siebren.

"I got to thinking, Hinka, if this should be Sister Anna's last night, and if I stayed here in a soft bed instead of going to her, I'd never forgive myself. So if you'll row me to the road, I'll go on tonight." He saw Siebren's face go wooden with tiredness. "No, you're to stay here. You're too tired to walk, and anyhow Anna's too sick for children and noise."

Aunt Hinka looked down at Grandpa's wet trouser legs. Grandpa looked down too. "I warmed up the coffee and dried off a bit beside the stove, so I'm fine inside and out, and I've got to go on."

"All right, but first Siebren must go to bed," Aunt

144

Hinka said. "You're a mess, David, but nobody will see you. I can't very well leave here now—Siebren here and my husband getting up to go to work in a couple of hours. But if it's really bad with Anna, promise you'll send for me."

Grandpa nodded. Aunt Hinka took the lantern. "We'll have to use this," she said. "We forgot to get kerosene yesterday in Lahsens, so there's just this and the ceiling lamp in the kitchen." She held out her hand to Siebren. She was actually going to leave him in this strange house alone with a giant deaf-and-dumb man. He didn't know of anything to say against it or how to say it. He looked around for the big ball, but it had rolled under the table and lay between Grandpa's feet. Grandpa looked impatient. Siebren took Aunt Hinka's hand and went with her.

They went down a long narrow hall between high whitewashed walls. The smoking lantern fumed back and draped shadowy wisps over him. The fumes made great giant shadows that edged and groped their way up the white wall.

"Couldn't I?" Siebren started to ask in a thin reedy voice. "Aunt Hinka, couldn't I ride in the boat with you and Grandpa—then you won't have to come back all alone."

"The boat won't hold three," she told him. But she must have guessed it was his uncle he was afraid of, for she said, "Your uncle won't bother you. He

145

seldom comes to the living room. The monastery's so big—it sprawls all over with halls and rooms—it's far too big for us. So years ago we built a sort of lean-to against the back of the monastery for us and our cow. It's a sort of kitchen-parlor with one closet bed and a shed adjoining for the cow.

"You see, your uncle works on the big farm that this monastery belongs to—this is the tenant house. He goes to work every morning at three o'clock, so he certainly doesn't take time from sleeping to wander around an old monastery."

"Goes to work at three o'clock?" Siebren asked. "But isn't it three o'clock in the morning now?"

"It can't be much after twelve. But, Siebren, if you're scared, do as you did in the marsh. Sing. Sing as loud as you want. Your uncle can't hear, and Vrosk will boom you company with the big bass drum in his throat."

Siebren made a little sound as if he'd laughed about Vrosk's big bass drum. His smothered sound was answered by a hollow cough out of a big dark room at the end of the hall. "That's Vrosk," Aunt Hinka explained. "He must be up on his booming stone, and he heard you—he's booming a welcome to you."

From the doorway Aunt Hinka called out to the frog in the well. Then Vrosk really answered. The whole dark room filled with sound. It seemed to bounce from the walls and run in rings and spirals around the black room. Aunt Hinka walked in with the lantern, and there in the dead center of the room was the big round cistern.

Aunt Hinka set the lantern on a loose blue tile that lay on the high stone rim of the well. The round wall had been built so high they had to climb up on a stool to stretch their necks over the rim and peer down at the frog in the well. There he sat—big, fat, spotted, and green—on a stone ledge just above the water. His eyes reflected red from the lantern light, and he looked like a puffed-up idol made of a green-jewel stone. He blinked up at them.

Siebren tried to pull and wriggle himself over the wide rim of the cistern to see Vrosk still better, but Aunt Hinka jerked him back. "Now you must promise me never to do that again. *Promise*. That well is all but bottomless. They even think it goes down into an underground river that runs under the marsh on its way to the sea where you live." In her earnestness, as Aunt Hinka turned to him her elbow hit the lantern and it rocked on the loose blue tile. The rocking light scared Vrosk. He jumped. "Now listen," Aunt Hinka whispered.

In the quiet it seemed moments before there was a splash as the frog hit the water. "Hear how far down the water is. Then below the water runs the blind river."

"Won't Vrosk be swept down the river?" Siebren whispered.

"No, he's wise enough to stay in the well where

there's enough light for him. There are stones that jut out every few feet along the inside circle of the cistern wall, so Vrosk swims to the one that happens to be at water level, and then he jumps from one stone to the next until he gets to the highest one, where you saw him sitting, for that's his favorite booming stone."

"Can't he jump out?"

"You mean jump in bed with you? No, the rim of the well is too high. But isn't it nice to have Vrosk here? If you get lonely, just talk to him, and when he gets back on his booming stone, he'll answer you. Vrosk and I talk a lot. Well, I've got to get going."

Aunt Hinka waited for Siebren to undress. After he'd climbed up the little stepladder to the high closet bed, she whipped up the ladder after him and tucked him in. She kissed him on top of the head the way Mother kissed Knillis. But Aunt Hinka sort of had to kiss him there, because he'd shot down under the covers up to his eyes to get away from the coming dark when Aunt Hinka took the lantern away.

"Just think—now you're sleeping in the big bed where bishops once slept." But then Aunt Hinka added immediately, "I'd leave the lantern, but it's our only one, and sometimes you need it badly in the marsh."

If he hadn't been so scared, Siebren would have been ashamed. She wasn't as big as he, but when she came back from taking Grandpa, she'd be alone in the awful black wet grassy marsh.

"Look," Aunt Hinka said, "I'm going with the lantern. But if you get scared—and Vrosk doesn't answer because he hasn't climbed back yet—then you just sing. I do that when I'm scared. When I'm too scared to remember a song, I make up the silliest song I can think of, because then I laugh, and when you laugh you can't be scared. So make up a silly song for me, Siebren—and tomorrow we'll sing it while catching that pike."

He nodded his head under the covers.

"All right then?" Aunt Hinka said. "I'll be back in a dozen or two songs, and I'll come in to see if you are asleep, and I'll leave you the lantern on the tile. But if you're awake and a little homesick or lonesome, I'll jump in bed with you, and we'll sleep and sleep until it's time to go catch that pike. . . . We'll just let your uncle sleep alone and be scared and lonesome without me."

It was such a funny thought Siebren laughed. But now Aunt Hinka was quiet. She laid a hand on him —he felt it through the covers. It was such a soft weight of comfort that Siebren lay still and tried hard to go to sleep for her. She must be waiting on top of the ladder until he went to sleep. He tried his best, but it wouldn't work.

He shot from under the covers to show her he was

149

brave and to tell her not to wait but to go with Grand-pa.

She wasn't there! She'd gone with the lantern! She'd gone so swiftly, so softly, he hadn't heard, and now everything was dark black—but the weight was still there! It pressed on him through the covers. He reached down and touched something cold and hard. He jerked his hand back and knew from the reek on his fingers that it was the blue tile for the lantern from the cistern's rim.

Aunt Hinka had laid her hand on him to keep him quiet. Then she must have run down the ladder and put the tile in place of her hand. It wasn't honest!

He writhed himself down. If he'd only stayed under and hadn't found out it was a tile. He couldn't touch it. He couldn't move it and its weight away from him; all he could do was lie and stare up in fright. Now he was really scared, and it didn't help to think of her small and brave out alone in the boat. His thoughts crawled—bitter like horror. Now he couldn't believe anything. He couldn't believe his big giant uncle wouldn't come—Aunt Hinka had said he wouldn't, but she hadn't been honest. Like all grown-ups she'd just said something to put him off and fool him.

Something in you knew it was meant to be kind, but that didn't help the part that knew it was to fool you. Siebren lay, trying not to breathe, trying to be so rigidly still that when the uncle did come, he'd think

150

Siebren was dead. But still the part that couldn't believe in Aunt Hinka was scrunched in the farthest cold corner of the great stone room—was squeezed in the corner, screaming with horror.

Dim lantern light came moving down the long narrow hall with its high white walls. It came fast—he couldn't move—couldn't get out of bed to hide in the corner or behind the cistern wall. The lantern threw huge shadows—it must be the giant shadows of the giant uncle. Siebren lay so stiff, so still even his lips went stiff. Then from inside him came a high whimpering sound.

From the doorway Aunt Hinka called out: "Oh, Siebren—not crying?"

He coughed to hide the whimper. Aunt Hinka whipped up the ladder with the lantern, and of course she saw his eyes were wet.

"Oh now," she said tenderly, "I merely ran out to the kitchen to tell your grandpa he had to wait until you were asleep. I thought you were nearly asleep when I had my hand on you, but so you wouldn't notice and wake up, I put the tile against you. My mother used to do that for me when I was a child—something against you for comfort—but all I had here was the tile."

Siebren raised up from the covers and gave her a weak watery smile.

"I'm going to leave you the lantern. I told your

grandpa we didn't need it with all those fireflies, and I didn't want you to wake up in the scary strange dark."

She was kind—but, oh, she was also honest! She was everything lovely and everything good. "It was the tile," he sobbed, leaning against her. "It was hard and cold and smelly from kerosene." Oh, it was a comfort not to be ashamed before her. He felt small. "Why do you have such a little boat?" he complained. "If it was bigger, I could go with you."

"Because I'm such a little person," she answered. "Your uncle is big and strong, and he has a big heavy boat. It got loose the other night and drifted across the marsh, but we won't need it to go fishing tomorrow. Of course, if that pike is too big, the little boat might go down with all three of us—but if he's that big, we'll ride *him* home."

She was *babying* him. He knew it—he loved it. "Aunt Hinka?" he asked to hold her there. "In that underground blind river down under the marsh are there even bigger fish?"

"I wouldn't know," Aunt Hinka said cheerfully. "I've never got around to fishing down there . . . I don't even know for sure there is a river. Some say it's just deep underground springs. Who's to know—way down there? Now see, I'll set the lantern back on the cistern. You'll be all right now, won't you? I do have to go, Siebren."

He had to keep her there a little longer. "Well, if

there *is* a blind river, then the fish in it are blind too, for if it's pitch black they can't use their eyes, and then they lose all sight."

"Wherever did you get such an idea? Blind fish!"

"I read it in a book. It was a wonderful story— scary wonderful!"

Aunt Hinka shook her head. "I would think so!"

"No, but," he persisted, "if we'd fish down the well with great long lines that could take our worms down into the blind river, then maybe we'd catch a big blind fish."

"Fish with worms in my well?" Aunt Hinka was greatly indignant. "That's our drinking water!"

"But you keep a frog in your drinking water," he argued.

"But Vrosk's a pet—not a worm! And frogs are so trim and neat in their tight green polka-dot swimsuits. Vrosk keeps the water clear of flies and mosquitoes and all kinds of crawly water-bug things. Besides—he's a pet!"

There wasn't much more to be said about that. Still, he somehow had to hold her; he couldn't let her go and be all alone in this awful stone room. Lying in bed, he was looking up at the ceiling shadowed by the smoky top of the lantern. Hey, there wasn't any ceiling in the big room. It was a barn of a room. They hadn't even known enough in those olden days to give a room a ceiling with an attic above it!

Why, he was actually looking up against the inside

of the slant of the roof! You could see bare beams thick as trees, and over the beams the rough lattice framework that the thatch had to be stitched to to keep it in place.

Siebren snorted out loud. "Why ever did they make your living room to look like the inside of a barn?" he demanded indignantly. Then he stared up again at the bottom of the tight gray-bronze-with-age thatch that had to keep out the rain. The beams were polished and smooth, but one of the stripped-bark trees that had been used for roof beams was split. A jagged piece had split away from the underside of the beam, and it stuck out—well, like his sore bandaged thumb.

"Aunt Hinka, look! That one beam up there is all cracked and split. It sticks out like a sore thumb."

"Child," Aunt Hinka said mock-severely, "you're not supposed to point out the defects when you're a new guest in a house."

"Oh?" he said, pushing the thought away down in himself to remember in the future. But now at least he had Aunt Hinka talking and staying a little longer. "It sticks out so—way up there," he chatted to hold her beside the bed. "It shows all over."

Aunt Hinka looked up at the flat splintered piece. "But didn't you know?" she said in most ladylike tones. "That's not a split beam—that's my clothes hanger. Whenever I sleep here in the big room with Vrosk instead of with my husband, before going to bed I hang all my clothes from that beam."

He almost believed her, she'd been so serious. Then he laughed out and wriggled all his delight. "You'd need two ladders to get there to hang up your skirts," he giggled.

"Oh no," she said. "Why, no. My big six-foot-six husband merely holds me up there, and then I hang all my clothes—most precisely."

Oh, she was big fun—oh, she was wonderful! That moment Grandfather threw open the kitchen door at the end of the hall and yelled out: "Now must this go on the whole night? Siebren, be still. You go to sleep right this minute."

Aunt Hinka looked as guilty as a scolded schoolgirl. "We did go on and on," she whispered. "You'll be all right now, won't you? I'd better go."

"Yes," he said. And for her he made the word round, firm, and sure. He sat up and nodded and nodded his head. When he was sure the kitchen door was closed behind her, he sang the one-line song he'd made up about her—"Old and knew." He sang it once going up, and he sang it going down: "Old and knew—old and new."

He sang it again because he loved her. Then he lay down. He felt so easy in his whole soft easy body that his whole soft easy body went sleepy. And the smoky lantern shone.

10

Blind River, Blind Fish

Siebren woke up and looked at the lantern. Had Aunt Hinka cleaned the glass? The room was much brighter than when he'd gone to sleep. He raised up on his elbow and looked toward the big round cistern. There was a splash. Oh, Vrosk must have jumped from his booming stone back down into the water. If only he hadn't gone to sleep, he and Vrosk could have talked back and forth. Now Vrosk was gone. Siebren tried a soft questioning frog croak, but no answer came from the well. Vrosk must be way down where the cistern rose out of the underground river.

Suppose the splash hadn't been Vrosk—suppose it

156

had been the swirl of a great fish with razor-sharp teeth that had grabbed Vrosk. There hadn't been a scream like the cry from the frog in the marsh, but maybe that was because the great fish from the blind river was so big that Vrosk had been swallowed in one awful gulp.

Had a blind fish come up in the well? Blind fish! Siebren stared at the lantern. . . . The big uncle was deaf and dumb, but *he* wasn't blind. He couldn't have heard him calling out to Vrosk, but he could see the light. Why had he wanted Aunt Hinka to leave the lantern? Now the uncle would see the light and find him.

If the uncle woke up—Aunt Hinka wouldn't be in the bed, so he'd get up and go looking for her. If he then opened the kitchen door, he'd see the light from the lantern. He'd come. He'd see him in the bed, but he wouldn't know who he was. He'd be so big, so tall his giant shadow would stoop into the closet bed long before he stood before the high bed and looked down at him.

He could scream, but the giant wouldn't hear. "I'm Siebren," he'd scream. "I'm Siebren—you're my uncle." But the man would look down into his screaming mouth and want to know what he was doing in the bed—and his wife not anywhere in the house.

Siebren couldn't think any further. What could he do? The door into the living room was the only door;

157

there was nowhere to run or hide. Could he hide down the well? Could he hang by his fingertips and lower himself to Vrosk's booming stone, and then go down the way Vrosk did from jutting stone to jutting stone until he was crouched just above the water? What then if the giant uncle lowered the lantern by one hooked finger from his enormous long arm, and the light fell on him crouched on a narrow stone above the water of a bottomless well—and the well above a blind, black river?

Could he blow out the lantern and take it down the well? But then he couldn't see either. He'd have to blow it out after he got down—could he do that? Siebren felt his fingers cramp—as if with the lantern hung around his arm his clawing hands were already digging into the mortar joints between the rounding stones of the cistern.

What if he fell? He couldn't swim. He'd go straight down to the underground river. There'd be a swirl, a cold dark splash, and a great fish would seize him. He'd squeal once like the frog in the reeds and be gone. Nobody would know, nobody'd care. The uncle couldn't hear; the fish wouldn't care.

Siebren shuddered away from his thoughts, looked at the cistern. No, he couldn't go down there—ever. Out of the dark came the clearing of a great hoarse throat. It came so suddenly after his awful thoughts Siebren shot under the covers to the foot of the bed and lay flat and breathless and quivering. Then he remembered. Why, that had been a sound that Vrosk made! It was Vrosk's first questioning croak. Siebren lay listening, and then the big stone room began resounding with Vrosk's mighty booming. Siebren scrabbled from under the covers to answer Vrosk. "Hi, Vrosk," he whispered. His voice grew stronger. "Hi, Vrosk, old frog. Hi, good old Vrosk. Hi, fellow."

While he was talking to keep Vrosk answering he slid out of bed, felt for the top of the bed ladder with his toes, and hurried down. Now he knew what he was going to do. He dragged the little bed ladder across the room and put it open, sprawling it in the hall doorway. Then he went back, blew out the lantern, and hid it behind the high cistern wall.

In the dark he felt his way to the closet bed, reached up to find the bed's edge, and shinnied himself up into it. There—there now if the deaf-and-dumb giant came, he'd fall over the ladder and maybe break his neck, but anyway he could jump out of bed and scoot past him down the hall while the big man still lay there.

Siebren lay spent, too tired to think one more awful thing. Then it came again—the clearing of the dry throat, but now he knew it was Vrosk. Siebren answered. His own throat was too dry to make much sound, but Vrosk heard and began booming again. It went on and on and on and on. It was so safe-monotonous sounding it was even making him sleepy. It was so safe! Suddenly Siebren was ashamed. He slid out of bed, dropped to the floor, found the bed ladder, pulled it back to the bed, climbed up it, and in grateful relief fell into bed. Vrosk was booming, the lantern was out—nobody would ever know the crazy things you could do if you scared yourself enough.

Oh, he was tired. It was late. It had been a long, long day, and now he was sliding down into sleep to Vrosk's endless booming. "Good old Vrosk," he whispered. "Good, good old Vrosk." It wasn't scary here now.

Siebren roused from sleep and lay staring. There was an allover gray light in the huge stone room. It must be day! Siebren turned on his back, stretched, and lay still. It was day, and he'd overslept when he'd thought he'd be too scared to sleep a wink all night.

Think of it—all Aal had was a cloudy little bowl with a few old two-cent goldfish, but he'd slept in a room with a stone cistern that rose out of an underground river. Think of it—he, high up in bed, but straight down from the middle of the room huge blind fish might have been blundering all night against the round wall of the cistern where it poked down into the underground river. Maybe in the dark the great fish had found the cistern's bottom opening and had risen to the very surface of the cistern's water. Maybe they'd lain there—only their tails and fins waving—listening to him mumbling in his sleep. But they couldn't get him; they couldn't even see Vrosk crouched on his booming stone. Then slowly with the coming of daylight they'd blindly sunk away—down to their black, blind underground river.

Siebren shuddered deliciously in his safety but then told himself to stop—you were really a handball of Satan if you played with making up things to scare yourself spitless. Wasn't it wonderful—daylight? So safe and all-seeing.

Luxuriantly, he twisted around. On the other pillow, pinned there with a safety pin, was a note. In the dimness of the closet bed he couldn't read it. He pulled himself to the edge of the bed, holding the note far out to see. Hey look, Aunt Hinka had brought a clock when she'd brought the note. There it stood on the lantern's blue tile on the cistern. He leaned out to see the clock.

Three o'clock! Wasn't that the time Aunt Hinka said the big uncle went to work? He listened—yes, the clock was ticking. But it must be wrong—it was daylight. He tried again to read the note, but with the curtains drawn the room was too dim. He let himself down as silently as he could and tiptoed to the window.

It wasn't daylight at all, and the clock was right. It was so light because it was full moonlight. It *was* three o'clock. If the uncle wasn't gone, he'd be up and

161

about right now. Siebren read the shaking note in his hand. He read:

WE COULDN'T LOCATE YOUR UNCLE'S BIG ROWBOAT. WE WERE GOING TO LEAVE IT ON THE FAR SIDE OF THE MARSH SO YOUR GRANDPA COULD GET WORD TO ME IF SISTER ANNA WAS WORSE. SO IT SEEMS BETTER TO GO WITH HIM NOW. IF THINGS AREN'T BAD, I'LL BE HOME IN THE MORNING. IF THEY ARE, I'LL HAVE TO STAY, BUT I'M SURE YOU AND YOUR UNCLE CAN MANAGE A DAY OR TWO WITHOUT STARVING. I TOLD YOUR UNCLE YOU'RE HERE—AND, SIEBREN, IF YOU DON'T WANT TO SLEEP THE COMING NIGHT IN THE BIG ROOM, ASK YOUR UNCLE TO SLEEP WITH YOU—HE'D BE PLEASED!

He wished Aunt Hinka hadn't mentioned the coming night. He stood, cold toes curling against the stone floor, looking out over the moonlit marsh.

A horrible jolting, retching, drawn-out sound came through the closed kitchen door down the hall. It rang and rang around the hollow room, fell silent and then it began again—a bawling, bellowing—a wretched lowing. Lowing! Why, it was a cow! It went on and on; it must be Aunt Hinka's cow. Was the cow loose in the kitchen? The sound seemed to come from right behind the kitchen door.

If the cow was loose, then the uncle must be gone—

162

but the cow would wreck the whole kitchen. Siebren moved into the hall, carefully calling out: "Where are you? What's the matter?" But the cow was still. Everything was still.

Siebren eased open the kitchen door. The cow was not there, but neither was the uncle. On the table stood an empty cup and a plate with crumbs. Beyond the kitchen the closet-bed doors stood open; the whole bed was empty. The big deaf-and-dumb uncle had gone to work. Oh golly, golly, golly—it was almost too much to believe. Siebren clutched the doorknob in his relief.

The cow must be in her own shed, built right onto the living quarters. Siebren opened the door to the shed, and a slate hanging there banged, but he paid it no attention for in the shed the cow began making huffing noises. Poor cow, she was lonely in this big house too. The open door let in light from the kitchen bed-quarters, and then Siebren saw the calf. The cow had just had a beautiful newborn calf! It was the earth's great miracle—early in the silent moon-bright morning.

The tiny calf couldn't even stand up yet. It lay in the straw while the mother made huffing, loving noises and licked and licked it with her big rough tongue. The cow was black, but the new calf was like a blond fawn, and the mother licked its soft-suede loveliness all dry and crinkly. Big-eyed, wondering, proud, the

163

cow looked up at Siebren but never a moment stopped licking her loved lovely baby.

As Siebren stepped back he bumped against the slate on the shed door. The whole big slate was full of fine spidery writing. Hey, it must be a note from his uncle! He read:

SIEBREN, YOUR AUNT TOLD ME YOU WERE HERE. WELCOME! I HAVE TO GO TO WORK, BUT OUR COW IS GOING TO CALVE, SO WILL YOU STAND BY FOR ME? IF SHE'S HAD HER CALF WHEN YOU GET UP, WILL YOU GIVE HER A PAIL OF WATER? WOULDN'T YOU WANT A PAIL OF WATER—IF YOU'D JUST HAD A CALF? DO THAT FOR ME, AND I'LL BE YOUR BIG DUTCH UNCLE—THE BIGGEST, DEAFEST, DUMBEST UNCLE THAT YOU EVER SAW.

That was the funny end of the note. Siebren laughed softly and gratefully. Then he looked for the pail. It stood in the dark part of the shed, rimful of water, and the wet rope by which the uncle must have dipped the water out of the cistern was still attached to the pail. Then the uncle *had* come to the cistern in the big room but hadn't wakened him. As he picked up the pail Siebren cringed with shame at the thought of the stepladder trap he'd put across the doorway so this wonderful uncle would break his neck. He was too ashamed of himself to be afraid of the cow—anyway she was tied to her crib with a rope. He lugged the pail of water to her and held it so she could drink. The cow sucked it empty in three noisy sucks.

At the sound the little calf came struggling up on its feet—unsteady, wide-sprawled, bug-eyed it forced itself up. Siebren dropped the pail and jumped to help the calf. With its trembling, clumsy legs the little thing would fall flat on its face. It tried so hard to stand that its big eyes popped out, and its little tongue stuck and stayed stuck between its lips. It stared and stared but without seeming to see anything.

His arms under the crinkly moist calf, Siebren lifted until its long legs stood straight. Little by little, and oh so carefully, Siebren let go, and wonder of wonders, the calf could stand. It was ten moments in the world, and there it stood—unsteady, helpless, foolish, beautiful. Here this moment, here this early morning was the earth's great miracle. Why, it was holy! And the cow mother went on licking her calf with the lovingest tongue in the whole world.

Siebren kneeled in the straw. He just had to hug the calf around its soft suede neck and lay his cheek against its cheek. Suddenly the great tongue of the cow mother licked over him. It was so rasping sandpaper-rough as it went up his neck into his hair that it almost took off skin and pulled out hair. Then the cow-mother boosted him aside the better to get at her calf.

Siebren lay flat on his back in the straw. From there

165

he again read the funny remembered thing on the slate: "Wouldn't you want a pail of water—if you'd just had a calf?"

Oh, he had to do something, he wanted to do something for his wonderful uncle and for the cow. He'd do things for his uncle while Aunt Hinka was away. He knew how to do almost everything around a house except wash and iron. He'd make the beds right now —even if it was only three o'clock in the morning.

He made a little joke to the cow. "If I were you and had had a calf that beautiful, I'd want three whole pails of water. Don't you?"

He grabbed the pail, flew to the cistern, and came panting back with a pail as brimful as his uncle's had been. The cow sucked it dry again in three great sucks, then shoved it aside to get back to the calf. Siebren flew again. But this time the cow could not be bothered with water—the little calf was drinking from her.

Siebren set the pail of water in the far corner. Then he started up the little ladder that must be for Aunt Hinka to get into the bed. From the top, he turned to look once more at the cow and the calf, saw the slate, and laughed out loud at its funny words. Oh, but it was wonderful here in the big house that had been a monastery! It was so safe that instead of making the bed he crawled into it—all unmade and frumped. He wanted to be in the bed of the biggest, deafest, dumbest, funniest uncle in the world.

166

The little suede calf had finished drinking and stood in wide-eyed innocence, as if looking up at him, while the mother licked crinkles and waves into his blond hair. Vrosk suddenly spoke up out of the well and asked his bullfrog question. The mother cow lifted her head, stretched her neck, and answered Vrosk in her high retched lowing. Vrosk boomed back, and the whole house resounded. But Siebren closed his eyes. Everything was safe, and everything was new, and everything was holy—this early miracle morning.

11

Fish Among the Lilies

Siebren woke, puzzled by a strong cow smell. He turned his sleepy, lazy head, and there through the open shed door he saw the black cow with her fawn calf lying thigh-tight against her. Finally he sat up— his stomach felt noon-empty. Oh, he must have slept a long time! Would his uncle come home for lunch? He didn't know—but there'd be nothing ready for him and nothing done in the whole house. Here he was, still in his uncle's bed at high noon. He shot out of bed and ran to the living room to dress. The clock on the cistern rim showed past noon—it was almost one o'clock. Siebren took a quick peek to see if Vrosk was on his booming stone, but Vrosk was down under the water where deep dark shadows rose, swirled, and sank away.

The clock had stopped, so it was even later than one. He dressed as if the house were on fire. Winding the clock as he rushed to the kitchen, he set about making lunch—lunch for himself, and for the big funny-nice uncle if he came.

It took time. He had to search for everything—even the plates, cups, and spoons. When it was done, all he had on the plates were two thick hunks of bread and cheese. The new bread had been hard to cut thin with the only knife he had been able to find. In fact, when he tried, he'd nicked his finger, so there was a bit of blood on one slice of bread. He'd kept that for himself, even though the cheese he had put on the bread would have hidden it. He worried that he'd cut the cheese too thick too—that would be wasteful and a sin—for the knife had been too big and too dull.

But there now stood the two plates with thick cheese on thick currant bread, each with a cup of steaming coffee beside it. He hoped his new uncle would let him drink a whole cup of coffee. He wasn't even sure whether his uncle came home or had his lunch at the farm. Still, lunch for two—two plates and two cups —seemed less lonely. It was so still in the house.

Siebren took time before sitting down to eat to push the outer door open wide, even though the smell of food and cows might bring in flies. In the whole flat sheet of marsh nothing stirred—no bird sang. He looked across the marsh, hoping to see his uncle coming, but there was nothing but a distant rowboat drifting, empty, oars hanging idle in the water. The rowboat made things seem lonelier. Siebren closed the door and sat down to his lunch.

The cow and the calf had gone to sleep, and most of the flies had drifted to the cowshed—they droned drearily there.

He looked at the clock—it said almost two. Of course he couldn't be sure how long it had been stopped. It was so quiet Siebren heard himself rumble with hunger. He bit into his bread. He remembered that he hadn't prayed, so with his mouth full he mumbled, "Lord, bless this food. . . ." Then he had an uneasy feeling—would it count against him to pray with a mouthful of food? Already he was eyeing the other plate and regretting that he'd given his uncle the thickest cheese. Cheese on currant bread—*ummm*—yummy!

What if Aunt Hinka stayed away for days? Currant bread and cheese was all there seemed to be in the house, and if they ate that three times a day, in a couple of days it would be gone. Then when Aunt Hinka and Grandpa came back, maybe a week later, they'd find two skeletons, his and his big uncle's. In the shed there'd be a black cow starved to leather who'd given her last milk to her soft, skeleton calf. He shivered deliciously, eating the delicious bread and cheese. Then with his mind carefully held on the skeleton playacting so it'd be as if he didn't know he was doing it, he grabbed his uncle's thick bread with the thick cheese.

He was so hungry he thought he'd never get filled. But when he'd finished every crumb, he was so full and the cheese had been so salty he drank first his own cup of coffee and then his uncle's too. He'd never had two cups of coffee before—somehow it felt sort of wicked. He waited for something to happen to him. Nothing did.

At last Siebren decided his uncle wasn't coming home for lunch. He decided he would explore the whole monastery. It was too hot and pressing outside to explore the island. He'd go down halls and into all and any rooms—he'd go wherever anything led—even down into tunnels under the ground that might lead to cells and dungeons where people had probably been tortured. Maybe there would even be skeletons lying in wet tunnels, half under water.

"No," he said sharply. Here he was doing it again—making himself a handball of Satan by scaring himself. "Get thee behind me, Satan," he said sternly. "I won't be a handball."

It helped. He wondered if saying it made Satan go away. He must remember to try it again sometime to see if it really worked. Hey, where was *his* Satan? He'd left the big black ball here last night, hadn't he? Oh— there it was, still under the table.

With the ball clutched against his chest, he went to the first door that didn't lead to the living room and the cistern. It opened to still another hall. Even down this hall he could hear Vrosk asking his bullfrog question. Then Vrosk began to boom. Oh, he *was* a comfort!

Siebren opened a door down the hall. It screaked out a high squealy ghost sound. There was nothing in the room, just bare walls of gray stone with white mortar between them. Siebren went in, and the door creaked shut. Then he saw it—in the far corner—a dead rat. It must have got into the stone room sometime when the door was open. Then the door had closed, and there was no way out.

The rat had tried to gnaw through the thick door that was studded with iron. It had broken one tooth— the tooth lay at the door, the rat in the far corner.

In its awful hunger the rat had gouged out mortar from between the stones. The rat's desperate teeth marks were everywhere, but it had starved to death. There it lay—a skeleton with a gray hide and a long straight dead tail. It was a mummy rat. Sharp, sour horror water ran around Siebren's clenched teeth. He

172

dropped the ball. It rolled over to the wall, bounced against a piece of tooth-chiseled mortar, and rolled back over the rat.

Siebren charged the ball, snatched it away from the corner, and ran. Behind him the door screak-squeaked slowly shut again. Siebren rushed headlong through the kitchen, past the table that still held the dirty cups and plates. Outside he didn't stop until the water's edge. He had to wash his ball in the endless spread of water, as if there could be no water enough. He had to be outside where things were big and wide and high and clean. He wasn't ever going to explore again.

There wasn't any clean cool air nor any wind. Over the whole marsh lay a stillness, a brooding, a threat. In the far reaches of water the reeds stood sullen, straight, and still. Siebren hunched down, washed the ball, washed it again, washed it yet again.

Across the marsh a bittern sent out its deep rusty-pump call once and was still. Behind and above him the house loomed somber. No little birds sang; not a bird twitted. Siebren shivered and thought of the rat. He never wanted to be alone in that house again. Once more he washed the ball.

He placed the wet ball behind a stump at the water's edge and began to run. He ran and ran, a hard stamping, pounding run. The ball was his marker. His heart pounded and his breath rasped as he circled the hump of the island a second time and neared the ball. He wasn't going to stop—he had to run. Something had to move in all this threatening stillness. Suddenly as he passed it he gave the ball a violent kick that sent it arcing into the marsh, but he ran on and didn't look back.

When he came around the tiny island once more, the ball was sailing away on the water. Then as Siebren stood looking the empty rowboat came slowly sliding around the far end of the island, oars hanging idle in the water. Now that it was near, he saw a long fish pole with its line poking out of the back of the boat. The boat rode as slowly as the ball but much closer to the island. It was almost as if something were moving it in toward the island—as if the boat had come for him. He waited.

The boat came slowly, but he had to take only a few deep over-the-Sunday-leather-shoes steps into the water to pull it in. He was going to have to go out in the boat to retrieve the ball. And here was a fish pole. When he had run around the islet, he'd seen a vegetable garden—there would be angleworms in a garden. He raced to the garden.

At the shaded end of the garden, under some low trees, was an old spade and beside it a small holeless flowerpot—just right for worms. But it was so close and airless under the low-hanging trees that after digging only a few spadefuls of earth, the sweat dripped from the tip of Siebren's nose when he stooped to pick up the worms.

174

The little flowerpot would hold only ten or twelve worms. Well, ten or twelve was enough. Siebren smeared the back of his mud-caked hand across his brow, listened in the stillness, then ran to the rowboat. He shoved the boat into the water, belly-flopped into the boat, and lay over the seat as the boat slid away from the island.

Siebren crawled to the middle seat, grabbed the fish pole, and pulled in the line. The big hook on the end of the line was blue-steel bare. He strung all his worms on it. There weren't twelve; there were only eight. Hey, but with a big hook and all those worms he sure ought to catch a big fish! Maybe the pike of last night! That's what he'd do. He'd go find the same reedbed where the frog had cried and try to catch the same pike.

When Siebren started to row, the hook, without any weight, ran just under the surface. It was a big safe-looking sturdy boat—not like Aunt Hinka's toy skiff —and he could row pretty well, he thought, for never having rowed before.

First he'd get the ball, Satan, back, but then he'd row so fast across the marsh the bait would go skimming and skipping and skittering on top of the water so only the fastest biggest fish could catch it. And that would be a big pike!

Pike were the fastest fish—except sharks, but they were in the sea. Sharks were faster than anything and could bite you into two pieces and swallow the two pieces whole. A pike couldn't do that—even though its mouth was filled, roof and all, with fine needle teeth.

There—he was doing it again—handballing—scaring himself. He wasn't going to think like that one thought more! But if he caught a big toothy pike, he wouldn't pull it into the boat with him. He'd row and row and drag the pike along behind the boat to the island. Then he'd take the pole, pull the pike up the slope, shove the butt of the pole into the ground, and leave the pike there like a staked-out cow until his big uncle came home. You wouldn't catch him putting his hand anywhere near a pike's mouth. No sirreee! Not him! Not on your life . . . no sirreee!

What about that? Boy, if it didn't make you feel big to talk big to yourself like that! "No, sir," he said aloud in the hot stillness, "no sirreee . . . not on your whole little life, Mr. Pike."

He reached the ball. With one of the oars he tried to flip the ball up into the boat the way Aunt Hinka had flipped it to him across the water. But the boat heeled and rolled, and instead of flipping the ball, the thick clumsy oar caught him under the chin. It hurt, and the ball swished away as the boat rocked. Whew, that had been scary!

Suppose the deaf-and-dumb uncle didn't want him out in his boat? Golly, if the uncle gave him a spanking, why, he was so big and strong he'd spank your fanny up into your stomach and your stomach up into

176

your throat. And he couldn't hear you yelling, so he'd go on spanking until there was nothing left of you—nothing to sit on at least. The thought was big-feeling and funny, and even sort of chummy. Besides, hadn't he got the boat back for his uncle? He sat there a moment and laughed, pleased with himself and his big thoughts.

Then he noticed that the ball was going the wrong way—past the end of the island, but not toward the shore where last night's pike bed had been. But the boat was going the same way as the ball even though he wanted it to go in the opposite direction. Of course, the boat was big and clumsy; the oars were heavy and unmanageable too . . . and, well, he'd never rowed a boat before.

Oh well—there'd be pike along this near shore too. Pike didn't just stay around one little old reedbed as if they were staked-out, grazing cows. No sirreee—pike were fast—pike went anyplace they pleased.

Siebren was proud when he managed the oars better and caught up with the ball. This time the ball rode past the middle seat where he sat and thumped alongside the boat. He grabbed at it with both hands, but the boat lurched sideways and tipped, and his hands and arms shot down into the water. Only the ball caught between his arms kept him from tipping out of the boat. He hastily slid to the safe middle of the seat and sat breathless with his ball.

In the shoreline straight ahead was a cove. It looked

177

deep and secret because it was shadowed with big trees. All around the cove were reeds, bullrushes, and great pads of water lilies—so many water lilies it looked like a solid field of blooming white. They were packed tight around a little open bay of black water. In the open water stood a colony of storks—white with black wings. The storks among the lilies almost looked like tall-stemmed flowers themselves. Tall giant flowers on long-legged stems.

The storks all stood one-legged because they were fishing, and they were so intent on their fishing they did not take fright at Siebren's approaching boat.

Then in all the waiting stillness the open black-water bay between the lilies suddenly boiled silver—boiled with tiny silver fish. They splattered on the dark surface and raced over one another, leaping, skittering, spattering in all directions. Siebren stood up in the boat to watch. The storks were too busy spearing little fish to notice him. The little fish hurled themselves toward the safety of the shadowing lily pads behind the storks.

Suddenly the storks themselves took alarm. They thrashed up out of the water—long legs dangling, they folded their legs up into themselves, rose slanting over the trees, and were gone. Siebren climbed up on the seat of the boat to see what was happening.

Into the shallow murk of water in the tiny bay came the shadow of an enormous fish, chasing and gobbling little fish as it drove them toward the shore. The flat lily pads stormed and heaved, but the storm was the big fish. Then the water died from its silver boiling and was black and still—the little fish all buried under the lily pads. In the tiny bay only the shadow of the great fish still circled. Siebren, up on the seat, stood rigid, watching as his boat slowly drifted into the little bay toward the lilies.

Staring at the fish, Siebren did not see his gob of twisting, wriggling worms entering the bay behind the boat—lifting, dipping. Suddenly the great dark shadow arrowed at the sliding bait. In the time of Siebren's one scared sucked-in breath, the fish had the bait. In the boat the long cane pole shivered, rattled, bent, then started to shoot out of the back. Without thinking a thought, Siebren threw himself from the seat onto the rushing pole.

The pole cracked under him and snapped in two —the top half of the pole flew out of the boat.

By the time Siebren picked himself up out of the bottom of the boat, the fish had darted out of the shallow bay. The broken yellow pole streaked on behind it as it headed toward the open marsh and the island of the monastery. The half-pole drove like a spear, now under, now shooting to the surface. It dashed and zigzagged on behind the terrified hurtling fish.

Too excited to know what he was doing, Siebren

grabbed the oars and began rowing after the hooked fish. He couldn't keep the boat straight. It was going toward the open marsh, but the fish had veered toward the island. But that was shallow water! The pole would get stuck, and the fish would break loose.

His eyes on the yellow streak of racing pole, Siebren was still aware of the big house on the island looming close. But there—there at the edge of the island stood a man. There stood his big uncle! Siebren jumped up in his circling boat and yelled and pointed toward the driving pole.

The man on the island made frantic down-motions for Siebren to sit down, then pointed to show that he had seen the pole. His uncle couldn't hear, but Siebren screamed like a madman about the great big fish —he'd get away, he'd get away! The man walked straight into the marsh and headed toward the fish.

The fish now was in shallow water near the island's end. The long-legged man went plunging and splashing after it. He took enormous steps. Now he was running, sometimes falling where the muck went too deep, but he always scrambled up again and went on —the man chasing the fish.

Siebren tried to control the boat's circling so he could go to his uncle and be of some help. After a while it did go a little better; he was aiming the boat truer; he was even nearing his uncle.

As Siebren got nearer, his uncle motioned for Siebren to be quiet with a finger to his lips. The fish had stopped; the cane pole lay motionless on the water. Maybe his tall uncle could see the fish, but the muck was deep here, and it was hard for him to stalk ahead and pull his legs out of the sucking muck without a sound. Slow step by slow step he advanced, but his feet kept sinking.

Then Siebren had a great thought—the ball! He sent it swishing toward his uncle. The uncle understood at once and grabbed the ball. Then, stooped over it, he stole silently ahead. At last he reached out for the shattered pole. Maybe the fish saw the reaching white hand for there was a sudden slashing of the water, but the uncle rose up in all his great length and with a roar of a splash threw himself on the fish. Then there was such a rolling, roiling splashing that Siebren could see nothing except the broken pole riding away.

The big man rose slowly up from the water but rose with the great fish squeezed in his arms. With its tail lashing, thrashing, the man still held on to the fish and came wading toward the boat, the enormous fish hugged hard to his chest. At the boat he took the butt end of the broken pole, stunned the fish, and threw it into the boat. It lay draped in all its great length over a seat.

Siebren's uncle, almost as limp as the fish, hung over

the back of the boat, catching his breath and spitting out water. At last he straightened up, and with a silent laugh over his face dug in his pockets until he came up with a piece of tailor's chalk. He held it up to show Siebren, then wrote on the back seat: "What a wonderful way for us to meet—with the biggest pike I have ever seen. So big we had to do it together. Hello, Fisherman Siebren—my name's Siebren too."

Siebren nodded and nodded. Then he just had to tell, tell everything loud and excited, even though his uncle couldn't hear. But he could see his uncle knew and understood—why, he must be reading his lips!

His uncle nodded along with his telling. When he was through, his uncle pushed him down on the seat with its wet milky writing from the wet chalk. Then he took the boat by the prow, and pulled him, boat and all, toward the island. But first he went in a wide circle to retrieve the ball. And golly, golly, but his uncle must know the swamp! Now that he wasn't chasing a fish and picking his way, he didn't plunge or splash or stumble.

Oh, it was the world's most wonderful ride—his big uncle, the biggest man he had ever seen, pulling him in a boat with the biggest pike that his uncle had ever seen. When Siebren looked down at the long, still fish he had to yell. He had to yell it out to all the marsh. "The biggest fish," he screamed out over the water, "the biggest fish. We caught him together, and we're going to eat him together. Uncle Siebren and me, Uncle Siebren and me."

It was as if the whole earth—all but his uncle—heard and listened and was silent.

12

Hunger Bones

When Uncle Siebren pulled the boat far up the slope of the island with Siebren still on the back seat, the sun was going down, and day was done. Lone and scary as the day had been, it had ended in greatness with the great fish. Now evening lay so quiet and brooding over the marsh it was as if the day were sulking because it was time to go.

. Holding the big fish by its gill, Siebren's uncle stood studying the sultry deepening sky. Then he made a sound that wasn't a word, but he made it to himself, and Siebren tried to look as if he hadn't heard. His uncle motioned for him to stand up so he could use the dry back seat to write on. "Something big's brewing up," he wrote. "This thunder weather will spoil the fish. You and I may be mighty fishermen, but even mighty fishermen have to clean their fish. Since it's your fish, I'll clean it. What can you do?" He cleaned the seat with a wipe of his arm and handed the chalk to Siebren.

"Make coffee and fry fish—Mother taught me," Siebren wrote. "Oh, the cow had a calf—and there is currant bread."

"I tended the cow, loved the calf, made my bed, and washed your dishes," Uncle Siebren wrote in turn. He gave Siebren a grin, looked at the sky once more, and walked away carrying the fish with three of his big fingers stuck up its gill. The fish was so long that even with the giant carrying it, its tail slid through the grass.

Siebren ran to the house. Oh, but he'd be busy frying all that fish!

At the end of the table Uncle Siebren set up an easel-blackboard that he had fetched out of a room down the hall of the rat. Siebren had not followed him nor told him about the dead rat. The fish slices were at the delicate point of turning a golden crisp —it was no time to talk about rats.

When the fish was all fried, Uncle Siebren brought a sealed jar and filled it with fish steaks to its neck, then together they went to the cistern and lowered the jar by a long cord deep into the cold water. The fish steaks in the jar were for tomorrow and the next day and the next—and they were for Aunt Hinka when she came back.

After the jar was lowered, Uncle Siebren reached down and placed a saucer of boned fish before Vrosk on his booming stone. Vrosk didn't take fright at all at Uncle Siebren's hand coming down to him. He didn't jump to hide under the water. No, he sat there and boomed and shouted about his meal of golden fried pike. It seemed right for Vrosk to shout about eating pike—maybe it was Vrosk's little frog-brother that last night's pike in the reedbed had swallowed. How many brothers did a bullfrog have?

Hey, when they got back to the kitchen to eat their meal of golden fish, he must ask his uncle that for a joke across the table. How many brothers does a bull-frog have? Sure, even if it had to be asked by black-board, it'd be like talking across a table.

They left Vrosk to eat his enemy.

Then he and Uncle Siebren feasted too. They ate and ate and then ate still more fish. It was wonderful greasy finger-eating, no woman's fuss, just plain, sim-ple, and fun. It was slow because the pike was full of forked featherbones, thin as pins, sharp as needles. He and Uncle Siebren leaned over the table, busily teasing the featherbones out of the morsels of golden fish. Siebren sat almost as high as his uncle because he was sitting on two silver-hasped Bibles with a towel tossed over them to sort of hide that they were Bibles. Siebren knew he could never tell Grandpa about it, but wasn't it wonderful that an uncle as big as his remembered from when *he* was a kid that a kid liked to sit high with a grown-up?

It was wonderful to think that if Aunt Hinka came home tomorrow—or even this night—there'd be a jar of fish waiting for her. Siebren didn't know whether to be prouder because he had caught the fish or because he had been able to fry it so well.

At last Uncle Siebren got up and wrote on the board, "Now before all this food overcomes us, shall we clean up? If your aunt should come home in the night, we'd want everything neat. If there is nothing to do, I know she'll go directly to Vrosk to greet him, and then she'll find the jar in the cistern, and she too will have a feast."

Siebren immediately began gathering the dishes, but he was dismayed. It looked as if Uncle Siebren planned to go directly to bed after supper. But then, of course, Uncle Siebren had been up and working since three o'clock this morning. But to go to bed at suppertime—couldn't they talk on the blackboard at least a little while?

Siebren wiped his uncle's writing from the board. Then he wrote, "I've got a little brother who can't talk—except one word—*Da*. Could you teach me to talk on my fingers so I could teach him?"

188

Uncle Siebren looked puzzled. He wrote, "For Pete's sake, why? If he can speak one word, he'll speak all words in time. And you can speak—so why, why in the world?"

Siebren answered, "Knillis could even sing at one time, but then he got sick, and now he can't talk or sing. So all there is to do is build blocks for him to knock down—over and over and over. That's all."

Uncle Siebren looked sad. He made a big impatient swipe with the towel and wrote, "Then build blocks for him—if it seems forever. Build them for him to knock down. You *want* to knock things down when you can't talk. But while you're building blocks talk to him. Talk and talk and talk—then after a while your little brother will talk too—if only to stop *your* everlasting talk." Uncle Siebren grinned.

Siebren grinned back, but he was ashamed and got right busy with the dishes. Uncle Siebren swept the floor. The house was quiet. Vrosk was quiet. In no time the work was done, and it was time to go to bed. Everything was clean but the blackboard. Uncle Siebren wiped it a bit with the flat of his hand and wrote, "This slate's as full of words as we are of fish, but slates can wait, and day is done. Shall we go to bed?"

Siebren rushed to the board. "May I sleep with you? PLEASE?"

Uncle Siebren erased it. "You'd rather sleep with

me than with Vrosk? I'm honored!" He smiled at Siebren.

They both grinned. Then Uncle Siebren folded the easel and started to carry it away. For a moment Siebren stood still—three o'clock in the morning would come, and his uncle would slip out of bed, and then later when he woke, he'd be alone in the house with a dead rat that was nothing but hunger bones. Siebren grabbed a piece of chalk and raced after his uncle. When he caught up, he tugged at the easel, wiped a clean place, and wrote, "A rat died in that room. Now it's nothing but hunger bones."

His uncle looked at him. Then he very deliberately wiped the whole slate clean. "This we'll take some of our bedtime for," he wrote. "Why is it that you're not afraid of tangling with a monster pike but are afraid of a long-dead rat?"

"The way it died," Siebren wrote.

"Why, when it's long dead?" Uncle Siebren asked on the blackboard.

Siebren thought it out. Then he wrote: "It wasn't awful to die the way the pike died—in a great fight —he had a chance, but the rat died slow and awful, to become just hunger bones."

Uncle Siebren nodded. "Hunger bones," he wrote. "That's a good way to put it. Yes, I understand. It had an awful death; we've come far too late to help, but would it help *you* if we gave it a fine funeral?

It didn't die right; would it help if we buried it right?"

Siebren nodded violently. Then Uncle Siebren put the easel down and motioned to him with a crooked finger. In the kitchen he went to the clock shelf and took down a cigar box. It was a beautiful cigar box, full of engravings and gold letters, and in the middle of all the gold was a sweet-faced woman. Uncle Siebren started toward the rat room with the box.

Siebren waited. He looked at the big Bibles he had sat on, and when his uncle came with the closed cigar box, he fell in behind him with one of the huge silver-hasped Bibles hugged to his chest. It seemed right, even if it was for a rat's funeral. It seemed to make up for the rat's awful death.

Uncle Siebren led the way to the fish-cleaning bench where he'd cleaned the pike. He lifted down a board, and there on the board he had nailed the head of the pike—maybe to show Aunt Hinka when she came home. Then Siebren, with the Bible, followed Uncle Siebren with the cigar box and the pike's head on a board.

This time Uncle Siebren went to the vegetable garden where Siebren had dug worms. He picked up the shovel and went to a little grass plot. There he dug out the sod and put the cigar box in the soft earth. The sweet-faced woman seemed to look up at them in approval. Siebren himself set up the board, with the great pike's head for a monument, while Uncle Siebren held the Bible. All was solemn. A little thunder muttered in the sky. A little lightning flickered, and as they returned to the house the first raindrops began to fall.

It was right that the rain should fall on the grave after the good funeral. And it was perfect later in bed when the rain began to clatter hard on the roof. There was nothing to be afraid of in the whole house. Siebren thought, and was somehow sure, that Aunt Hinka would come home in the night. Then everything would be perfect—perfect.

Much later when Siebren wakened he was alone. He felt for his uncle, but the place beside him was empty. But at the moment of waking, his mind also knew that the rat was no longer in the house. The rat had had a fine funeral.

The cow beyond the open door sighed a great sigh, but it was because she was heaving herself up onto her feet so that her little calf could drink. Siebren looked at it. The calf was hardly bigger than a dog— not nearly as big as Landsake, he idly thought. Suddenly he sat up. "Wayfarer," he said aloud. He'd forgotten Wayfarer! He'd completely forgotten the little dog from the moment he'd come to the marsh and the monastery.

"Wayfarer," he said again. "Hunger bones," he said slowly.

Wayfarer, locked up in an empty school, would become that too—hunger bones—starved bones with some loose skin lying over them!

Oh sure, he'd written a smudgy note to his father on the school door, but what if it had rained? If it had rained even the least bit in Lahsens, the writing would have run down to become a little smudge puddle on the stoop of the school.

What had been wrong with his mind? Even if it hadn't rained, he'd never thought that his father might not come to the school—his father was also putting up other buildings in other villages, and he and his men might not have come back to Lahsens at all the next day.

Now it was the second day after the night he had locked Wayfarer in the school. The time had gone with catching the pike, the wonderful evening with the new uncle, and the rat funeral, and he'd never once thought of Wayfarer. If poor little Wayfarer was without food, without water . . . by this time he'd be too weak, his throat too closed from thirst, to whimper out so passersby could hear him. By this time he would have crawled into a corner—like the rat. He was lying there becoming hunger bones.

It was all because he, Siebren, was a handball of

Satan. Satan had made him do these things. In the stark silence he admitted it—he *was* a handball of Satan. He'd given Knillis the rusty sickness in his head. But he'd been younger then. Now, a fourth-grader, he'd done it again—again he'd made himself a handball. Now because of him a little crippled dog that had trusted him was thirsting and starving in a closed empty school.

"Stop it!" he said fiercely. The words hissed out of the bed and went on and on into the dark reaches of the whole house. He lay there hoping Vrosk would hear and begin booming. Vrosk was silent, but now Siebren seemed to hear a faraway thin crying as if a small girl were crying—or the ghost of a little dog! Had Wayfarer already died? He was so little, so thin, so crippled it wouldn't take long for *him* to die.

"Stop it!" he screamed. "Stop it, Satan."

Now Vrosk suddenly boomed out in answer. He boomed on and on, but the thin crying sound had stopped. No, there it was again under the booming. But that wasn't crying! It was someone answering Vrosk. It was—it must be Aunt Hinka! Aunt Hinka was back. Aunt Hinka had come in the night!

Siebren dropped from the edge of the bed and started to run as soon as his feet hit the floor.

It was Aunt Hinka! She'd hitched herself up on the broad rim of the cistern. The lantern was beside her. She was leaning on one hand, far out over the

194

well, talking to Vrosk. Siebren stopped—he'd come on bare feet in the dark—if he scared her now, she'd fall in the well. He backed down the hall as far as the kitchen, then came back singing the song of the frogs with wooden shoes. The cuckoo, funny song wouldn't scare her.

Aunt Hinka was smiling as he came through the door. "That's nice to wake with such a happy song. I've been crying. Sister Anna died. I didn't want to wake you with my crying, so I let you sleep and came in here to cry it out with Vrosk. But now I'm done, and do you know I'm hungry. I forgot to eat yesterday."

It was wonderful, her saying that. He swung up beside her, found the cord, and pulled up the jar stuffed with pike. He opened the jar and held it out to her. Aunt Hinka saw at once that the thick steaks were pike. She was amazed at their size. Oh it was wonderful because Aunt Hinka tried to believe he'd caught such a giant pike, but she hardly could.

Siebren sat beside her, trying to prove that he really had caught such a fish. "I can show you the head. Uncle Siebren nailed it on a board, and we used it for a monument to a rat. I'd show you now, but you've got to wait until it gets light."

Aunt Hinka had stuffed her mouth full and was going "MMM . . . mmmmmmmmm."

"Watch out for the featherbones," he warned as if

she were a little girl. But then it was *his* pike, so maybe it wasn't too old-mannish for him to warn his little aunt. She nodded, but she had already teased tiny featherbones out of the next morsel and held it ready to pop into her mouth.

Then Siebren took a piece of fish too. He didn't eat it; he just held it, because holding it made him feel sure and easy with his aunt. Holding the fish, he began telling her right out about Wayfarer. Aunt Hinka listened. Then it was easy to tell her about Knillis and how his little brother had a sore rusty head because he, Siebren, had taken him to play on the rusty rails. After that it was still easier to tell her about the miller of Nes, who—Grandpa had said— talked queer and did queer things because he was a handball of Satan. And then at last he asked her right out—was he a handball of Satan too?

All the time he talked Aunt Hinka did not look at him, just munched thoughtfully and carefully sorted out featherbones until there was a little gleamy pile on the rim of the cistern beside the lantern. She did not say a single word, and she did not have to because he could see she was thinking hard. She gave little nods and made little murmurs to herself that showed she was listening and thinking seriously.

Oh, it had never been so easy to talk to anybody! Maybe it was because Aunt Hinka was as small as he.

196

He didn't have to look up to talk to her. You had to talk to other grown-ups that way, and then you felt small and helpless, and without enough words—sometimes so helpless it made you shake. But then the grown-ups said you were throwing a stubborn tantrum.

Aunt Hinka only listened. Then he was finished. And he felt so easy and empty inside it was almost like when you were hungry. He bit hungrily into his piece of pike—and he wasn't even very cautious about the bones, he felt so light and good. They munched together.

His little aunt went on eating too—she didn't begin talking and giving easy answers to show she was a grown-up and knew everything. At last she wiped her mouth, then she thoughtfully looked at her hand. She fished in her pocket for a handkerchief and carefully wiped each finger. She studied one wiped finger, held it up to the lantern, and licked it. She seemed to be thinking only about her fingers. Then she held her finger up and said, "Number one, that thing of thinking and saying and doing queer things making you a handball of Satan . . . well now, you've heard me talking and laughing to Vrosk, telling everything to a green frog. Now having heard that—and it's pretty queer—you say right out to me: 'Aunt Hinka, you are a handball of Satan.' "

Siebren jumped down from the cistern to stand before his aunt as if he had to see her better, as if he couldn't believe what she had said.

"Say it right out," Aunt Hinka ordered. "You say, 'Aunt Hinka, you're an old, old lady; you play in the marsh, talk to frogs, talk to yourself—you even sing foolish songs you make up for yourself. Oh, what an awful handball of Satan you are!' "

"I can't say that! It isn't true." Siebren shook his offended head. "I won't! You are *not*—you are wonderful."

"Well, you are wonderful too," she said. "Oh, yes you are. See, it *has* to be, because we are so alone. I live in a marsh with a deaf-and-dumb husband, you sit endless hours with a baby brother who can't talk, so both of us have to make up things within ourselves —for ourselves. If that's what your grandfather means by a handball of Satan, I for one am glad to be a handball. It's fun. It's fun because you're always surprising yourself."

Siebren kept nodding his head, speechless because he was so grateful. He was a whole bubble of light airy happiness. He was a bubble.

"All right," Aunt Hinka said, "now let's take number two. She held up two fingers, saw they were still oily from fish, and licked them both. "Number two," she said again. "That's Knillis, the little brother with the rusty head. Could your head rust?"

Siebren shook his head.

"Of course not, it's flesh and blood—and I suspect some bones too."

Siebren giggled.

"Now then, unless Knillis was a metal baby when he was born, Knillis can't rust. If that sounds funny, it isn't any more funny than making yourself believe that Knillis got a rusty head from playing on rusty rails. *You* haven't a rusty head, so Knillis didn't get it from you, and he didn't get it from playing on rails. It has nothing to do with you. You've done nothing but good for Knillis by sitting with him. You've only helped. Believe it—it's true."

She waited a little. "Three," she said. "Number three—now I'm going to be stern. I don't like it either—what you did to the little dog. You're right there; you thought only of yourself, not of his welfare. The day after tomorrow is Sister Anna's funeral, so your grandfather won't be going back for three days. If your father didn't let Wayfarer out and nobody came along, your little dog will be in hideous thirst—and thirst is a hundred times worse than hunger."

Siebren couldn't say a word—his throat was too full, and his eyes were watery.

"But Siebren, do you think your deaf-and-dumb uncle would let a dumb animal suffer like that—he dumb himself? Do you think I would? I only hate pike. Well then, tonight when your uncle comes, we'll tell him. We'll have a quick supper, and then your uncle will put you on his shoulder, find his way through the marsh, and carry you to Lahsens. If Wayfarer is still there, he'll carry each of you on a shoulder all the way home to Weirom. He's going to do that anyway, with or without Wayfarer, because your mother will worry and wonder why you are staying so long." She made a zero with two of her fingers. "Number nothing . . . all done. Now is everything all right?"

Siebren leaned against her and nodded. Oh how he loved her—how everything bubbled within him—oh, he was a bubble of happiness!

Then Aunt Hinka jumped down from the cistern and said, "Look, it's getting light, so let's get out to this pike's head. He must be the biggest ever caught in this marsh, and I've caught some lunkers. But one thing's sure: I've got to see a pike head on a tombstone for a rat. And then, while we're there we'll dig some worms and go fishing. We'll catch some pike, sing some songs, and have fun—you and I have been through such awful things. The cow's had a calf; you've caught a pike, but I've had only sorrow."

"Aunt Hinka," he said softly, "I've prayed to go fishing with you." It was too much for him to say more. He turned and ran down the high narrow whitewashed hall to the kitchen.

13

Monastery Balm

A queer glassy yellow light fell into the kitchen as Siebren opened the outer door. Behind him, Aunt Hinka stopped and stood listening. "Did your uncle pull his boat way up on the shore last night?" she asked.

"Oh yes. Almost to the house."

"Well, I didn't pull mine up. Let's do it fast. Do you hear that?" Again she stood with head cocked, listening.

"Isn't it thunder?" Siebren asked. "Last night it thundered way across the marsh too."

"It's more like the rumble of a thousand bulls," she answered, mystified.

"It's trains."

"Trains don't come through swamps. There isn't a track within thirty miles of here. This seems to be coming through the ground, as if you can hear it in your bones. Let's get the boat up fast."

Behind Aunt Hinka he hurried to the boat, but he kept his head tilted to the faraway sound. Aunt Hinka was right; there was more than sound—there was pressure, there was threat, and an unearthly sullenness. The sound kept coming. The faraway roar now slid toward the marsh.

"It's still dark," Aunt Hinka said. "Yet there's a queer light around the edge of the dark. Listen, there isn't another sound but the roar. It's as if everything has hidden—we'd better hide too." They got busy with the boat. The two of them panted and struggled, but still it didn't want to move up the hill. "There isn't any air," Aunt Hinka gasped. They gave up and stood waiting. You couldn't put it into words, but you knew something was coming—there was a hollow dread that kept growing in the distance and in you. Suddenly Siebren couldn't stand it. He broke away, ran to the kitchen, found the big ball, and ran with it back to his aunt.

It broke the spell. "No, Siebren, don't do that again. We mustn't part—not even for a moment." Then Aunt Hinka stiffened and grabbed him. "See—see—there . . . it's a tornado! Run!" They raced for the house. Over his shoulder Siebren saw a cloud of roaring blackness tossing like an evil monster in the swamp. Then the long, twisting, snaking snout of the monster dipped down, and there was a hideous watery sound as it sucked up the water and made itself a dry path through the swamp. He was too frightened to tell Aunt Hinka; anyway there was no air to talk —or breathe.

"I don't know where to go," Aunt Hinka gasped.

With a thunderous clap the kitchen door sucked shut before their faces; behind them came the black roar. Aunt Hinka grabbed Siebren and ran past the closed door and around the corner of the house.

She clung to a windowsill and flattened herself against the wall of the house. Siebren clung to her and clung to the ball. Then the roar came over them, and a great shrieking, screaming blackness rose as the tornado took hold of the house. The house twisted and wrenched. Aunt Hinka flung him to the ground. The ball flew out of his arm, but amazingly it went up like a released balloon—it bounded up along the house wall. Then Aunt Hinka was dragging him backward by the heels around the corner, and they both lay flat behind the house.

The tornado dropped all the water it had sucked up out of the swamp down on them. In the next shiver of a moment the monster sucked the water up again and almost lifted them up into itself, then a different darkness settled down upon them. Now there was no roaring, no wind—only darkness. Both on their knees, they stared up. The new darkness was the roof; the whole roof was lowering down over them. Against the roof's ridge the black ball bounced between the roof beams until it pressed up against the thatch.

The next second it was total blackness, and water dripped on them from the inside of the thatched roof. The ball fell down behind Siebren and bounced away. On hands and knees he crawled mindlessly after it. In the wet he felt a sleazy soaked cloth under his hand, thought of snakes, and squeaked out, "Aunt Hinka, are we dead?"

"No, the roof from the living room came down over us. The tornado pulled it off the stone walls, but it was too heavy to hold; still, the suction must have been so strong that the roof let down gently. The edges must be settled deep in the wet ground, and that's why we see nothing at all. There's no window —and a good thing, for that tornado ripped my clothes over my head so hard that my ears are bleeding—it hardly left a stitch on me. Otherwise I'm untouched. Are you all right?"

"Everything's all right," Siebren answered, "even my clothes—I'm just wet." He poked around and got the wet cloth that had felt like a snake. He wrung it out for her. "Aunt Hinka, here's a skirt or something." He could hear her teeth chattering.

"Cold and wet," she complained. "Awfully cold and wet, but not dead. No, we aren't dead. By some great mercy we came through unharmed. It was the water coming over us that kept us from going along with the tornado. But, oh Siebren, I'm afraid that when the tornado lifted the living-room roof it sucked up the water from the cistern—and Vrosk with it. Vrosk in the sky!" She cried a little.

Siebren sat in the wet. Aunt Hinka cried jerkily as she crawled about searching for her clothes. "We wouldn't have to search for things if you'd had little windows in the end of the gable roof—as we have at home," Siebren said somewhat resentfully as he searched for the ball. He found it, held it tight for a moment, then he put it down and sat on it to get out of the sopping wet grass.

His eyes were beginning to get used to the darkness; now he could see Aunt Hinka near the far end of the roof. "I can see you," he announced.

"Thank goodness we *didn't* have any windows in the roof ends," she said. "Thank goodness I've got my clothes on now. They're cold and wet and nasty, but it was good to be busy—and not think."

Siebren could see her standing. He got up and brought her the ball to sit on and stayed close, his hand on her shoulder. She reached up and held his hand. "We're a pair of lucky ones," she whispered, "for handballs of Satan. Bless those monks for building that roof so solid and heavy. They did us well—those thousand years ago. Bless them."

"When will people come to help us out of here?" he asked.

"I don't know," she said. "I'd like to think soon, but the marsh is such a big lonely place that even a tornado could thrash about in it, and only the fish and the frogs and the birds would know. If it wasn't seen from the farmhouse, there might be nobody until your uncle comes from work tonight—and that's twelve hours away. It all depends on what path the tornado takes after it leaves the swamp."

"What will we do?"

"What can we do? The roof weighs tons, and all the edges are settled deep in the soggy ground. Oh, I do wish I knew how the cow and its newborn calf fared."

"The boats went up into the sky," he told her. "I saw them. Their anchors floated straight out behind them. One boat caught in the top of a tree—and then the tree went up."

"I saw fish in the sky, and there was a path through the swamp as wide as the road to Amsterdam," she marveled.

They were silent for a moment. "We're alive," they all but said together.

"Maybe we'll soon believe it," Aunt Hinka said and squeezed his hand.

"If we could dig ourselves out and see everything, then we could believe it," Siebren said.

"Let me think," Aunt Hinka said. "Remember the beam that had split? Remember I joked that it was there I hung my clothes? Of course, I weigh nothing, but together maybe we could pull it down and break it away. Then we'd have something to dig under the edge of the roof, and maybe we could crawl out."

Together they searched in the dark and found the split beam. Now that the roof was not on its walls, it wasn't so high. Aunt Hinka leaped and grabbed. Siebren leaped, and together they hung, face to face. "Jump and jiggle and bounce," Aunt Hinka ordered. "That might do it."

The split plank-like piece slowly bent, but it was so tough it swung them upward toward the beam before their jouncing made it bend again. "Now," Aunt Hinka breathed, "now kick like mad—kick."

The split piece groaned. There was a tearing sound, and they fell together on their backs on the soft wet grass, somehow managing to hold the split piece of wood away from their faces with their four hands. "We did it!" Siebren yelled. "Now where do we dig?"

"Anywhere," Aunt Hinka said. "In this marsh there are no stony places—only muck."

It did not prove to be true. Again and again wherever he tried, Siebren struck rock.

"Of course," Aunt Hinka said. "The monks just left

the rubble when they built the monastery. Of course."

She took the board from Siebren. "Let's try the far end." She stamped with her foot and prodded with the pointed end of the board to find a place where the sod was thickest. Suddenly she rammed the pointed board so hard it stuck in the sod and stood up like a broad spear. Siebren took his turn. Then he felt it strike something hard and solid. He dropped to his knees, and digging like a dog, he pawed the sod and earth away with his fingers. "Aunt Hinka! It's something smooth and flat—it looks like the stone cover of something."

Aunt Hinka dropped beside him. Together they tore away the sod and dug away all the dirt that covered the flat stone. It was round. There was a thick rusted-iron ring set in its center. They tugged at the ring, but nothing happened. "It's too heavy. Get the ball," Aunt Hinka said.

They worked the point of the board into the ring and placed the ball under it, then put all their weight on the far end of the board. They bounced themselves up and down. The big ball squeezed half flat; then slowly the round stone began to yield, slowly it lifted. They twisted the board on the ball, turned the stone cover away from the hole, and let it fall onto the grass. Aunt Hinka stooped far into the round opening. "It's so dark, but it looks as if it might be the opening to a tunnel. I don't know . . . would there be a tunnel under the monastery? Why? Did the monks make tunnels to hide from enemies? Siebren, if you could lower me. . . ."

"No," he cried in terror. "What if it isn't a tunnel? What if it's a bottomless well?"

"Yes, that could be too," she said. "Maybe it was an outside cistern before they built the one in the living room so the monks wouldn't have to go outside for their water. Remember, our forefathers were still fierce heathen tribesmen. Why, it isn't twenty miles from here that they killed the good St. Boniface, who tried to convert them." She tugged the point of the board out of the stone cover and poked it down the hole. It struck bottom—hard bottom. "Siebren, it *is* a tunnel. It's solid down there." She swung herself down; her fingers clutched the edge a moment; then she dropped out of sight.

Above, Siebren kneeled and peered. His little aunt spoke up. "I've crawled a little way straight ahead. It's a tunnel, and it's clear. It's musty and damp—but no water. Come down, and we'll explore."

Without a word he let himself down into the tunnel.

On the tunnel's floor they crouched and peered into the darkness ahead. Siebren felt something and put out his hand. It was the board his aunt had poked down the hole. He pushed it ahead, sliding it over the floor.

They listened to the board scrape-grinding along. Then Aunt Hinka laid a quieting hand on him, and crouched close together, they listened in the silence. "Of course we've got to explore," she whispered. "A tunnel just can't stretch out before you while you sit and look at each other. We've got to follow it. We'd never like ourselves again if we just stayed here, we'd be so ashamed. Yet somehow it scares me, living here nearly all my life, and all that time a tunnel under me." She was silent a moment. "Not that we're not going," she said stoutly, aloud. Then she whispered again. "We'd better go on hands and knees. It could suddenly plunge down; there could be holes, even cisterns . . . good land, I'm whispering again. Whispering—when there's been nothing down here for a thousand years."

"We could push the board out before us," Siebren said. "Then, if there was something, we'd touch it first with the board."

"Yes, and roll the ball ahead so if there were holes or wells, we'd hear the splash."

"We could even use the board as a bridge to crawl over holes," Siebren said. But he didn't move.

"That's thinking," praised Aunt Hinka. "Now let's us two handballs stop handballing! Let's stop scaring ourselves, or we'll never move." She got up. There was a purry whispering as the big ball she'd been sitting on began to move down the tunnel. Siebren licked his lips and croaked out, "The tunnel must slope; the ball rolled away."

210

"Of course, that's it," his little aunt agreed almost too eagerly. Then she laughed. "Tell me, Siebren, am I a child? I can't get going. When you shoved that board down the tunnel, I heard things grit and roll, and I thought of bones. Maybe in a wet swamp the monks would have had to be buried here—under this hill they made. We'd be among skeletons, bones rolling under our hands. Ugh."

"I felt it too when I shoved the plank, but I reached down—it's only gravel and round stones—just like on a road."

"Of course," Aunt Hinka said. "The noise you hear is me kicking myself under my skirts. Me and my imagination! Of course they would have laid down gravel, otherwise every time they came down here, they'd be crawling around in muck and sludge. Of course!" She snorted at herself like a little pony. "What wouldn't I give for a little light—or a little courage. . . . Come on, let's follow the ball. If the tunnel stays wide enough, we'll crawl side by side so we'll touch each other, and we'll keep pushing the board along—it will feel out whatever's ahead."

They began to creep, sliding the board out in front of them. "Why, good sense says," muttered Aunt Hinka, "that this was an escape tunnel leading from inside the monastery, so that means there's got to be an opening that leads up into the house. All right? Shall we believe that? Then forward march—on our knees." She chuckled. "Charge!" she ordered, "but at a crawl."

Siebren had to laugh. They inched the board ahead. It ground and grated. Siebren scraped up a handful of gravel and pushed it into his aunt's hand. "See, it's gravel, not bones."

"Sure, sure," she replied. "What else? Unless it's gold. Now why couldn't I have imagined gold instead of bones—it's just as easy. And why are we crawling? For all we know we can walk."

She must have risen to her feet as she said the words, for up above him Siebren heard the explosion of a muffled cut-off cuss word. "Thunder-Tomcat!" she said bitterly. She dropped down beside Siebren. "Those monks crawled," she told him. "And we crawl. I won't be sassy again—I really hit my head. Stupid little idiot," she scolded herself. "Hardly any body and even less sense."

Siebren snickered. It was good to hear her. It took away the solemn dread of all the centuries that seemed to stand waiting in the silence.

Then as they crawled along, Siebren's elbow bumped something. It moved away, touched his ankle, and was gone. Siebren found his aunt's ear and whispered, "Something moved. I felt it. It's behind us."

"Wasn't it your ball?" Aunt Hinka said right out, loudly.

Siebren could almost hear his tense muscles sighing as they sagged back into place. Of course it had been the ball—nothing else moved like that. He twisted around—if it was the ball, it had to be right near them. It wasn't.

"I'll wait here while you find it." Aunt Hinka was back to whispering again. "I'll block the tunnel so nothing can pass me."

Siebren swung around to crawl back, but his shoulder grazed no tunnel wall. He put out his hand. There was an opening in the side of the wall. Had the ball gone through that? "Aunt Hinka, there's an opening; there's a hole here leading out of the tunnel." Now he was whispering too.

He waited until she came. Together they felt along the edges of the opening. It seemed to be a small arched doorway. If it was, it was no bigger than the opening to a dog's kennel. Then Aunt Hinka crawled right through. It scared Siebren. He sat still.

"Siebren, where are you?" Aunt Hinka said. "I felt something move, so I crawled in—I thought it was you. Where are you?" She sounded scared.

"It was the ball," he said. "You touched the ball, and it rolled away. I'm back here in the tunnel."

"Siebren, come here." Her voice was suddenly excited—she wasn't whispering. "I'm in a little room. I can stand up. There are shelves all around me—I can feel them—but they are empty—no bags of gold." She laughed.

Siebren crawled through the opening. "There is too something here," he said, "right on the floor. It's a jar. A crockery jar, it feels like. It's closed—it's sealed." He wrenched at the narrow neck of the jar. In the darkness something broke away from it and shattered on the floor. It was the neck of the jar; he'd wrenched the whole neck off. At once the dank little room was filled with perfume. Aunt Hinka smelled it too. "Lovely," she said. "Perfume—spicy perfume— oh nice! What is it?"

Siebren poked his finger down in the jar. The tip touched something smooth, soft, greasy. "It's grease," he said, "but nice. I think it's a salve—a nice-smelling salve."

"Salve?" Aunt Hinka stooped down beside him. He put the jar into her hand. "Lovely," she breathed. "Agh!" she exclaimed, and spat. "I tasted it," she explained. "It's salve all right—tastes like medicine, but it's nice to smell."

There was a little silence. Then he heard her sniff and sniff. "Oh, I remember that smell," she said. "My grandmother had a jar of salve that smelled like this. Balm, she called it. Monk's Balm, I think. No—Monastery Balm! That's what it was. Why yes, that's why the monastery was here in the swamp—for the marsh herbs from which to make the balm. My grandmother said it was famous in her day—a miracle salve. It was sent all over Europe, for all sorts of wounds and sores."

"Sores?" Siebren said. "Then it's for little Knillis.

That's why I found it—for Knillis's head. It was here all the time, but there's some left for Knillis's head."

Aunt Hinka laughed. "No, Siebren. I scarcely think a tornado came and ripped the roof off our house just so you'd find something to cure Knillis's head. Think of all the damage a tornado causes—it's a big price for one jar of salve." Her voice was kind and calm and reasonable.

"But the doctors don't know how to cure it," he argued, almost violently. "Pieter Klimstra's salve won't do it—this will. I know it will. I know!"

"Then believe it. I'll believe it too," Aunt Hinka comforted. "Let's believe it, because it's already done *us* a lot of good. Nothing's scary anymore. Isn't it funny? Just one homey little jar of salve with a nice smell and nothing's scary. . . . So that's what this tunnel was for—to store and preserve the balm they made. No doubt it would keep almost forever in this damp closed air under the moist marsh earth."

"Imagine finding it for Knillis—a miracle to find the miracle salve," Siebren said slowly, as if he hadn't heard one word she had said.

"Come on," she said, "let's find the other opening that must lead up into the house. We can come back some other time with light and explore, but now I want to see what's become of the house and Vrosk and the cow and the calf."

"Will you bring the ball?" he asked. "I've got to

carry this broken jar." Without another word, he crawled out of the little room, down the tunnel, and over the board. He didn't bother to take it along. There seemed nothing to fear now. They just had to find some chink or splinter of light that would show where the tunnel led up into the house.

"Not so fast," Aunt Hinka called. "I can't crawl very fast in these long skirts. Can't you wait? That salve has kept for hundreds of years—it ought to keep a little longer."

No, he couldn't wait. Clutching the jar, he crawled ahead. It was as if he'd found the treasure of all the ages. He couldn't wait. He had to find light. Suddenly around a sharp turn in the tunnel he could see light ahead. "Light," he yelled, "there's light."

It was just three pencil-thin strips of light making a half-moon circle, but it was as if the sun had come blazing up.

"Where do you suppose that is under the house?" Aunt Hinka asked him. They scrambled side by side toward the pencil of light as if they were having a race. Aunt Hinka poked the ball out ahead of them. Then the ball hit the half-moon of light, the three bars of light quivered, and the ball came bouncing back. "It's loose—the light quivered," Aunt Hinka said. "It seems to be a loose stone in the wall that must be the end of the tunnel."

Siebren put the jar of balm behind him for safety.

Aunt Hinka was already at the end of the tunnel, struggling with the stone. She had her fingers in the lighted crevice. "I can stir it, but I can't pull it back," she said excitedly. "It seems to wedge. I held my eye to the crack, but all I can see is another wall straight across. What can it be?"

Siebren peered through the crack. "It's a round wall—like a tower," he told her. "Like the cistern."

"The cistern!" Aunt Hinka cried. "That's where we are. We're looking through the crack around Vrosk's booming stone . . . this is the round stone right above Vrosk's booming stone—I know it by its shape because the mortar was gone from around it. But it's wedge-shaped—we can't pull it toward us."

"Could we push it?" Siebren asked. As he asked he pushed hard at the stone. Suddenly the whole stone slid ahead, and there was a splash far down in the cistern. Aunt Hinka shoved Siebren aside and pushed her head through the opening made by the fallen stone.

"Siebren, Vrosk's ledge is still sticking out into the cistern." She was silent a moment as she stared around. "You can see the stone bottom of the cistern—there's so little water left. That's what happened. When the roof went, the tornado sucked all the water out of the cistern, held it against the roof, and let it down on us behind the house. That cistern is deep—deep, but there's no underground river. The bottom is loose stone." She let Siebren poke his head into the hole to look. "Would you dare stand on Vrosk's booming ledge and then pull yourself up over the rim of the cistern? I can hang onto your legs—but would you dare?"

"The stone looks real solid," he told her. "Look, it's so big it's part of the tunnel. You're on it too, so it wouldn't tip. It's solid."

"Yes, I see—but would you dare?"

"If I don't look down, I can. It isn't far from the rim. We reached down to it when we gave Vrosk some fried pike. But don't hold me too tight; I've got to be able to get my arms up over the rim."

Siebren lay on his back and inched through the hole until he was sitting on the booming stone. His legs were still in the tunnel. Aunt Hinka held his ankles. "It's funny, looking up and seeing the sky— with the roof gone," he said shakily. "Well, now I've got to stand up. Just hold me by my belt as soon as I'm up."

It worked! He scraped himself up the cistern's inside wall. "It's not far now I'm standing up," he told her. "Now let go so I can swing up and over."

Aunt Hinka's head was in the hole. She looked up at him dubiously. Then she let go of his belt. Siebren scrambled up over the rim and stood in the living room looking around. "Aunt Hinka," he called down, "there's nothing—nothing—just sky. Not a chair, not a thing. All the covers—even the mattress is gone—

just bare bed boards . . . Aunt Hinka, Aunt Hinka—there's Vrosk in the bare bed! Right on the bed boards —right in the middle like a stone frog. Oh, and the jar with fried pike must have been sucked up out of the cistern with Vrosk, and it went into the bed with Vrosk. It isn't even broken, but the lantern lies smashed."

"Run! See about the cow and calf."

He ran through the gooey, sticky muck the tornado had left—it went all the way down the hall. He had to butt the kitchen door with his shoulder again and again before it opened, but then the whole kitchen lay there before him undisturbed—cups and plates neat on the table. He dashed to the shed and wrenched its door open. The black cow was pulling hay down from her crib; the little calf was butting its head up against its mother to get her to let down more milk to drink. Siebren closed the door softly.

All the inside doors had been slammed shut, but the outer kitchen door now stood wide open. When Siebren looked out, the marsh lay with its sheet of water, silent and flat as it had always been before. Only across the far marsh was there the destruction of uprooted trees, roots tangled and poking up into the air. That moment a figure came plunging through the uprooted tangle, came plunging straight on into the swamp. It was Uncle Siebren! He came plunging, sinking, falling, but always he pulled himself up again by sheer wild, mad strength, and always he came on.

Siebren leaped from the doorway and ran toward the marsh, waving and yelling and screaming. At last Uncle Siebren must have seen him, for he wildly waved; then he came on faster and wilder than ever.

Siebren tore back to the living room, yelling and yelling, "It's Uncle Siebren; it's Uncle Siebren— straight through the marsh . . . the cow and calf are fine . . . it's Uncle Siebren!"

Aunt Hinka was standing behind the cistern. She had to take time to shake her skirts down. "Thought if I got rid of you and tied my skirts around my neck, I could come up over the cistern like you. Ain't I all but as big as you are?"

"It's Uncle Siebren," he shouted, "straight through the marsh—like the tornado!"

"Ah, boy—ah, but then he s safe from the tornado too . . . but straight through the muck! Oh, he's got to see me to know I'm safe. I've got to run and show myself. Siebren, bring Vrosk. Cup him in your hands and come." She came around the cistern and ran from the room.

Siebren leaped for the closet bed, grabbed the high edge, flung himself up, grabbed up Vrosk, and with the big motionless frog in two hands, leaped down to the floor, and ran after Aunt Hinka—down to the island's edge.

Aunt Hinka stood, waving. Uncle Siebren saw her,

and he waved, stopped, and shook both hands high above his head like a triumphant fighter, then came on again, but he slowed his desperate plunging.

In Siebren's warming hands as he and Aunt Hinka stood waiting, suddenly it happened. The bullfrog's eyes flickered; its mouth came open. It uttered a small feeble croak, opened its mouth as if to croak again, but closed its eyes, and went to sleep in the cup of Siebren's hands. And that way they waited for Uncle Siebren.

14

Miracles in a Row

They were talking—Aunt Hinka and Uncle Siebren—
their eyes fixed on each other. Their fingers must be
making letters, and words were flying. Oh, it must be
wonderful to make your fingers talk! There wasn't a
sound.

They were all sitting on the rim of the cistern.
Siebren was between them, and Vrosk was quiet and
warm in the cup of Uncle Siebren's big hands.

Siebren looked at his own fingers and made mo-
tions with them, but it was meaningless. Then in
twisting them his thumb suddenly hurt. His sore
thumb! He'd never thought about it all day. But now

223

he wouldn't have to wait until he got home to see if the Monastery Balm would work. He'd try it on his own thumb. He gave the dirty blackened bandage a hard wrench to make his thumb even sorer. He slipped the bandage off—yes, his thumb was bleeding a drop. It looked sore, even if it didn't feel very sore.

With the bleeding thumb Siebren thought he could interrupt the two in their soundless talk. "Aunt Hinka, my thumb's bleeding. We left the salve and the ball in the tunnel. Could Uncle Siebren swing me down so I could get them? Then I can put some balm on my thumb, and we'll see if it really works."

Aunt Hinka smiled as she looked at his held-up thumb. "I was just telling your uncle that we need to get you home, and about the little dog in the school-house. But you know what he told me? News came to the farm where he works. The tornado went through Lahsens and did nothing but lift the roof from the new schoolhouse. Then it went on to Nes, missed the village, but just outside it took the top off the ages-old windmill, and the miller was up in his mill. Just think, your uncle knew nothing about all this. He was working in the barn because of all the rain, so he saw nothing and, of course, he couldn't hear even a tornado. But one of the men who brought the news said it was a senseless tornado that did nothing but take off the top of a tumbledown mill and the roof of a school, besides thrashing around uselessly in our marsh. Your uncle can read lips, so when he read that, he tore out of the barn and ran all the way here. Then when he got to the edge of the swamp and saw our roof gone, he says he lost his mind and just plunged straight through the marsh. He says he doesn't think he breathed until he saw you in the doorway. Imagine, a schoolhouse roof and an old mill —if it didn't take the miller with it—and our roof. It only touched down in those three places. Of course, there may be much more that the men didn't know."

"The miller of Nes," Siebren said. His lips were white and stiff. "The tornado took him. If he went with his mill, then Wayfarer went with the school."

"Siebren, you don't know that!" Aunt Hinka said fiercely. "You just don't know. You don't even know your little dog was in the school. Your father may have taken him home safe and sound. You don't know. You *can't* know."

"Aunt Hinka," he begged. "May I go home? Now, right now?"

She looked at him questioningly.

Slowly Siebren squeezed the words from dry lips. "Grandpa said the miller of Nes was a handball of Satan."

Aunt Hinka, tiny and sweet, uttered a fierce unladylike snort, pushed her hands behind her, and came flying down to the floor. She turned on Siebren almost angrily. "Yes, your grandfather said that—but didn't we agree that we were handballs too? Yet that tornado set the roof down on us so gently we weren't hurt at all. And because the roof did come down over us, we found the miracle balm that is going to cure your little brother. . . .

"And of course you're going home—now—as soon as your uncle is rested a bit. But do you know why you're going? Because all kinds of rumors about that tornado will fly. They'll probably hear that our roof came down and smashed all of us . . . it's that way with rumors. Your parents will worry themselves sick. And you are worrying about your little dog and that miller, and most likely none of it true.

"But Siebren, Siebren—if it turns out not to be true, then will you believe? Then will you believe in miracles and not in handballs of Satan—not anymore —*ever?*"

He looked at her with love—the little woman, so big with wisdom. He trusted her. He nodded and leaned his head against her. Then he asked, "May I take two pieces of the pike home with me? Else my father will never believe I caught such a fish." Oh, how he loved her!

"Of course," she said gently, "but you must take the whole jar." She turned to Uncle Siebren, and her fingers flew. Then she turned back to him. "Uncle Siebren says you're going on his shoulders, but the tornado has changed the marsh—all the paths he knew —so all he can do is blunder through the same way he came. You may both go down in the muck and the water again and again. Then what would happen to your fish and the Monastery Balm?"

"Couldn't we go in one of the boats?"

"Remember?" she said. "Remember you saw them go up in the trees?"

He thought and thought. Then he asked, "If we slit the ball open, put the two jars in, and sealed it again, then even if we go down, the ball would float—wouldn't it?"

"Is the salve that important to you?" she asked. "More than the big proud ball?"

Siebren nodded, but he was somber. "If Wayfarer went up in the tornado, then all that's left is the miracle salve."

A slow cloud in the sky drifted across the roofless room. Aunt Hinka looked up at it. "But the salve is for Knillis; the ball is for you. Is it that the salve is another miracle?"

Siebren thought it out. "Well, finding the salve because the roof came down on us and kept us safe would be two miracles, wouldn't it? Could another miracle come so soon? One miracle after the other?" He so wanted to believe—he had believed, but now was it too much—had he wanted too much?

Aunt Hinka stared up at the slow cloud. "I guess you mean that a miracle isn't easy. It has to push so much away that is everyday, ordinary, and school-day dull. Do you mean it's so hard that there can only be one once in a great while—just one at a time?"

"I guess so. Yes, that's what I mean."

"Let's ask your uncle," Aunt Hinka said. "People who have to be silent all their lives think deep. I know he believes in miracles—so much that he's still waiting for the miracle of speech. He doesn't so much mind not hearing, but to tell things with one little old soft rag of a tongue instead of ten clumsy fingers—" She broke off; her own fingers were flying as she talked with her husband.

"I asked him," Aunt Hinka started, then suddenly pointed to the empty window. Across the torn marsh the sun was beginning its morning blinking, and there in the sunshine swam a mother duck with her long file of ten yellow ducklings. Not a bird called in the silence, but where a tornado had been, ducklings came.

"I asked him," his aunt began again, "could there be a whole row of miracles—one coming right behind the other—like that row of ducklings behind their mother? He said, 'Why not? If one miracle breaks through, isn't it that much easier for the next to follow—the way that mother duck breasts and breaks the water for the ducklings to swim in her wake?' He asks, 'Why must a miracle come alone? And who knows what is enough for you?' But he warns you that a miracle can't begin to happen unless you first believe in it. He says that's the only part *we* can do —believe, only believe."

Siebren looked up at his uncle with eyes of wonder. He softly repeated, "Who knows what is enough for you?" Oh, but Uncle Siebren, who had no words, was wise—as wise as Aunt Hinka.

Uncle Siebren stepped down from the cistern, lifted Siebren, then held him down until his hands were on Vrosk's booming stone. Then Siebren slid through the hole into the tunnel. He handed up the jar and then the ball. Then his uncle reached down and swung him back up onto the cistern's rim.

In the kitchen Aunt Hinka had started heating red sealing wax. She had carried Vrosk with her. Now he sat on the table, but he was still. Uncle Siebren set the ball and the jar of balm beside the motionless frog. He reached up to the clock shelf and took down the narrow box that held his straight razor. Siebren watched, and he bled a little inside when his uncle cut a swift slice into the black glossiness of the ball. He was thankful his uncle had done it for him, for it would have been like cutting into himself to cut the ball.

Next Uncle Siebren took the big cleaverlike knife and chopped the narrow broken neck of the jar off clean so Aunt Hinka could put a dollop of hot sealing wax into the stubby neck for a cork. But before she did, Siebren poked a finger down into the salve; then he smeared it over Vrosk's back. Right then Vrosk hopped the whole length of the table—eyes flickering, mouth opening. Of course there was no way to know

229

if the miracle salve had done it, but Vrosk *was* hopping. And he *smelled* lovely—a spicy green frog.

"You see," Aunt Hinka said, "one dab and he hopped, and his eyes came open. You see?" Siebren loved Aunt Hinka for saying that. Uncle Siebren was holding the gash in the ball open wide, and Aunt Hinka lowered the jar of balm with its red sealing-wax cork down into the ball; then she put in the glass jar with the fried pike.

"Oatmeal!" she exclaimed. "Nothing can break in oatmeal. We'll pour the whole ball full." Uncle Siebren held the ball open for her, and she poured from a big farm bag until the ball was full of oatmeal. After that she poured a long smear of hot red wax over the gash in the ball to close it and seal it airtight.

While the wax cooled and hardened, Uncle Siebren swung Siebren up on his shoulders. Then he stooped so Siebren could kiss his little aunt. She kissed him and said, "Now you be back soon—we haven't caught a pike together yet, and we need to find all the mysteries of the whole marsh. You come back and back and back, because miracles come with you—I think because you are a little miracle yourself."

"Aunt Hinka," Siebren's voice was husky—the parting was coming so suddenly—"Aunt Hinka, I love you, I love you. And I love Uncle Siebren. I love the marsh, and . . . and everything. . . ." His voice trailed off, and he swallowed hard.

230

"Yes," she said. "I know, I know. So you come back real soon." She handed his ball up to him. "Rest the ball on your uncle's cap. Don't worry if you take some spills. You can get the ball back if it falls, and everything inside it is safe and soft-tight in oatmeal."

Uncle Siebren stooped through the door and went at a dogtrot straight to the water. At his splashing, the mother duck hastily rounded the end of the island with her little brood of flowing, yellow ducklings.

Siebren could only yell good-bye, good-bye, without daring to turn to see his little aunt again. If he did he would cry. Uncle Siebren slipped and plunged, but he always managed to keep from going quite down. At a great pace they headed toward the far shore of the marsh and the awfulness of the uprooted trees sprawling up into the sunshiny sky.

Almost in no time the swamp was behind them— now, there ahead was Griet's house. But when they came to it, it stayed closed and still. No Griet and her shotgun, no clumsy calf of a Landsake came bursting. The house seemed to be waiting. The swamp had lain waiting too. Only the deaf-and-dumb giant moved in long strides across the waiting world. It was as if it were waiting for him to come fast on the big shoulders of his big uncle. But maybe it was the little dog in the school that was waiting for him. He hoped so.

Siebren hoped with head down because he was afraid to look. If Lahsens was destroyed and the school gone. . . . Then Uncle Siebren was walking on cobbles, and the cobbles were Lahsens. He wouldn't look—he couldn't look, for if the school was gone, that would end his hope. He stared down at the cobbles.

Then without slowing, his uncle turned into the house-store of the dike inspector. Siebren couldn't help it; he raised his head. There stood the school, but it stood without a roof and without its boarded door. The tornado had come to the schoolhouse.

Uncle Siebren shoved the store door open, and the bell rang. He lowered Siebren to the showcase, still piled high with its pyramid of balls. The tornado had taken Wayfarer away, but the pyramid of balls was undisturbed. It wasn't fair.

Aal came through the drapes at the sound of the bell. She threw up her hands when she saw Siebren. She shook hands with Uncle Siebren very politely because he was deaf and dumb and she couldn't talk to him. Uncle Siebren made a motion to him.

Then Siebren said, "Oh, Aal, Uncle Siebren wants me to tell you Grandpa's sister Anna died, and the funeral is tomorrow. Aunt Hinka would like you and your husband to come. And the tornado lifted the roof off the monastery—just like it did off the school next door. . . . But Aal, the night I was here, I locked a little dog inside there for my father to take home the next morning. If he didn't come, and the tornado came, and Wayfarer was still there, he went up with the roof. But I did it—I locked him in."

"What did you say?" Aal asked, not hearing or understanding. She plumped down in the little velvet chair, and she was so big it creaked. She looked down. "I shouldn't sit in this," she said confusedly. "Siebren, do you know what that tornado did? It was a monster of meanness. It took the roof off the school, but it whirled all the dirt from the school and the yard into our store. I've only got a little part clean; my husband can't help—he's gone into Weirom even if he *is* retired—because do you know where your father's school roof is? It's smashed against the dike at Weirom. But all this soot, and all our new goods covered with grime. . . ." Aal smeared a hand over her tired face.

Then Siebren asked, "The miller—the miller of Nes—what about him and his windmill?"

Aal shook her head. "I've heard nothing, but I've been so busy . . . plaster and dirt and dust over everything."

"Are the goldfish all right?" Siebren suddenly asked.

"Goodness—I've been so busy I never thought of them. They must be choked in dirty water!" Aal jumped up so quickly the chair arms still clung around her. She paid no attention, raced to the window. Uncle Siebren jumped up in alarm; he and Siebren ran after her.

In the thick plaster-coated water one goldfish floated

233

on its side; the others were on the bottom trying to breathe with round mouths wide open. Aal grabbed the teapot from the table and with her hand skimmed the thick dirt off the surface and dumped it in the teapot. The dead-looking goldfish stirred and floated into her hand. She stared at it and began to cry. Uncle Siebren grabbed the teapot and looked around. Siebren guessed he wanted clean fresh water, so he flew to the bathroom. When he came back, Uncle Siebren took the little fish from Aal and dropped it into the fresh water. With his big finger he stirred the water in the teapot into a little storm, and the 'dead' fish rode the storm ahead of his finger.

"I didn't think," Aal mourned, "and now my goldfish is dead."

"I didn't think either," Siebren answered her, "and now the little dog I locked up is dead."

Aal sniffed and wiped her eyes. "Well, but aren't they in heaven now?"

"Only people go to heaven," Siebren told her.

"That's what people say," Aal said dully.

"What do dogs and goldfish say?" She began to cry again.

The goldfish in the globe that Aal had skimmed clean came to the surface and began making clabbering sounds with their round kissing mouths. Aal stooped over them, crying, and in the room there was no sound but the goldfish kissing up at her. That's

234

all there was in the whole world—a kiss from a gold-fish.

Uncle Siebren nudged Aal's elbow and pointed down at the teapot where the water was swirling. But now the goldfish was moving feeble fins, swimming on its side and sometimes swimming right side up—but swimming.

"It's a miracle," Aal cried. "He whirled my gold-fish into life again. It's a miracle!" She pulled Uncle Siebren's face down to her and kissed him. With the teapot in his hand he had to let her, but he got red over his whole face. He shoved the teapot at Aal, grabbed up Siebren, and fled.

Aal, stooped over the teapot, hardly noticed they were leaving.

Siebren grabbed the big ball as they passed the counter. Then Uncle Siebren thought better of it, went back to Aal, and leaned Siebren down so he could kiss her. Siebren kissed her, but her mouth was a little fishy from the kissing goldfish. He told Aal good-bye.

Siebren looked at the schoolhouse as they passed. The yard was sucked bare of everything, and the school was nothing but bare walls. Next would come the windmill. There it would stand, awful—topless and wingless—and the miller gone with the tornado.

Now there in the flatness rose Nes. But there—

there rose the windmill. There it was! It was whole; its wings were turning.

"The wings are turning!" Siebren yelled and pointed. "It's got all its wings, Uncle Siebren."

Maybe Uncle Siebren just felt it, but he looked as if he'd understood. He went at a dogtrot to the mill. Maybe the miller had heard too, for he poked his head out of the same little oval window and looked down. "Back is it, my young wayfaring friend?" he called down. "Riding high, isn't it? Riding high with a big black ball. I'd say Napoleon himself on his snow-white charger never rode finer. And did the trip bring you good things—not only a tornado?"

"Even the tornado," Siebren called back, "even the tornado brought a miracle."

"The tornado a miracle?" the miller called. "Well, the tornado bypassed Nes; it passed hard by the windmill and did it no harm. Well, I guess that's a miracle too."

Uncle Siebren had kept walking, and now they were past the mill. Siebren called over his shoulder, "May it fare you well, miller of Nes."

Out of the oval window the miller called, "And may it fare you well too, my young wayfaring friend. May everything fare you well."

Then they were on their way to Weirom. But now there was hope, oceans of hope, for there had been a miracle. The tornado had not come to the miller of Nes.

Long before Weirom, Siebren saw the dark mass smashed against the green dike, and the dike was black with people. Uncle Siebren had seen it too for he kept his face turned toward it, but he did not go there. Siebren was thankful, for Wayfarer might lie dead among the dark twisted lumber.

The goats of Japik Maaikus heard Uncle Siebren, and they bleated out a weepy welcome. It sounded sad. Everything would be sad if Wayfarer was gone.

It was even sadder when they came to Peppermint Street, for there was nobody home. It must be that Father was at the dike with his smashed roof, and Mother must have gone with him. There was no one to greet them.

Then Uncle Siebren pushed the door open, and Siebren called out, "Knillis? Knillis—aren't you here either?" But there Knillis sat, tied in his high chair, his little hands mittened. He stared up at the big man coming in. Siebren put the ball on the tray of the high chair.

Knillis stared wide-eyed at the big glossy ball, bigger than his whole little head. Siebren ripped the red wax away, and the ball yawned open. Knillis's mouth puckered to cry, but Siebren pulled out the jar with the Monastery Balm. He pried the wax cork from its neck, and with two fingers he dug a rich dab of the

238

balm and rubbed it into the rusty spot on Knillis's head. Knillis didn't cry, didn't even twist away; he just sat cooing at himself reflected in the shiny ball.

Siebren stepped back. Of course he didn't know how long it would take the salve to work—but he could hope. Then from behind the big ball Knillis looked up and spoke a word. *"Sieb,"* he said. He said it again, *"Sieb,"* plain and clear.

Knillis had spoken! Knillis had spoken his name! In the surprised quiet that fell, the front door burst open and Mother came running. She didn't take her shoes off—she came right into the room with her wooden shoes *on.* She grabbed Siebren. "Oh, Siebren, Siebren, safe and sound. Through a tornado—but safe and sound."

Siebren held up the jar. "Mother, the tornado came and took the roof of the monastery, but it brought us the Miracle Monastery Balm. Mother! I put it on Knillis, and then he said 'Sieb.' Knillis said 'Sieb.' Did you teach him to say it?"

Mother shook her head. "No, if he said it, he said it of himself—he missed you, Siebren. Oh, but he missed you!"

Mother was so astonished that only then did she remember her manners and shake hands with Uncle Siebren. But she talked right up to him—oh, she must know that Uncle Siebren could read lips.

"I saw you from the dike," she told him. "I ran

back to yell the news to Siebren's father. He's coming . . . oh, here he is."

Father came pounding in from the hall on his wooden shoes.

"Take off those shoes, you, you—" Then Mother looked down at herself, saw her own shoes, and laughed and laughed.

Father had made so much noise Siebren hadn't heard the click-clack of toenails on the linoleum in the hall. But there, right after Father—just as ordinary as everyday—Wayfarer came into the room, the white bandage on his leg.

"It's Wayfarer . . . it's Wayfarer," Siebren screamed. "But he was dead! The tornado smashed him and the school against the dike. And he was dead because I locked him in the school. It's the miracle; it's the miracle."

He grabbed up the little dog and held him close. "It's Wayfarer, Wayfarer—to the end of all our days."

Father picked up Siebren—Wayfarer and all—and held him high up toward the ceiling to hush him and make him less screamy. "Hush, son. Hush, son. What's all this yelling? Didn't I do just what your note on the school door told me to do? Is that the miracle? All it was is that I'd forgotten some blueprints I needed, so late that night I came on my bicycle to pick them up—maybe not more than an hour after you put him there. I read your note by my carbide light, put the dog and the prints in the bicycle basket, and pedaled them home . . . it's as simple as that. Are miracles that simple?"

Siebren looked at his father and said, "But Aal didn't know you came, so I knew Wayfarer had gone up with the roof and was smashed against the dike."

"Aal didn't know. They'd gone to bed, so I didn't disturb them. And there, son, is your great miracle."

He loved his father that shivery moment, but miracles were not to be poked fun at. "Oh no," he said severely. "Oh no, Dad." He pointed to Knillis's shiny, spicy head and then to the jar of Monastery Balm. "The tornado brought it. Aunt Hinka and I found it in a tunnel under the monastery. It *is* a miracle, and it's going to cure Knillis's head."

Uncle Siebren had read his lips, for as Father set him down his uncle put a big approving hand on his shoulder. Then Father shook hands with Uncle Siebren. Siebren told him all about the tornado and the roof that came down over him and Aunt Hinka and how they found the tunnel and the Balm and the way back up through the cistern to the roofless house.

"Now *that is* a miracle," Father said to the giant uncle. "And any man that brings my son back whole out of a tornado gets a roof over his head if I have to lift it there piece by piece. For that, any school roof can wait."

Uncle Siebren had read his lips, and he grinned

and nodded. Father was already getting some big pieces of sketch paper out of his desk. "We'll have breakfast," he announced, "and we'll tell each other everything. You've had a hard journey, and we've had a hard time at the dike. With notepaper and lipreading we'll talk it out. But already I know that instead of a wagonload of school roof, there'll be a wagonload of men and Uncle and I riding back to that monastery where my son and his aunt went through a miracle. Now *that* was a miracle! Come on, son, and we'll all have breakfast."

But Siebren said, "May I stay here, Dad? I want to stay and wait for the miracle to come to Knillis's head."

"Of course you must," Mother said, "for only then will it come, for always there's a lot of hope and a lot of faith and love mixed up in a miracle. Of course, you must wait with Knillis."

At the sound of his name, Knillis looked up from the glossy gleam of the big ball and loudly said, "*SIEB.*"

And there was a little bit of oatmeal mixed in the shiny perfumed salve on his rusty little head.

HARPER TROPHY BOOKS you will enjoy reading

The Little House Books *by Laura Ingalls Wilder*

> Little House in the Big Woods
> Little House on the Prairie
> Farmer Boy
> On the Banks of Plum Creek
> By the Shores of Silver Lake
> The Long Winter
> Little Town on the Prairie
> These Happy Golden Years

Journey From Peppermint Street *by Meindert DeJong*
Look Through My Window *by Jean Little*
The Noonday Friends *by Mary Stolz*
White Witch of Kynance *by Mary Calhoun*

Harper & Row, Publishers, Inc.
49 East 33rd Street, New York, N.Y. 10016